LARKSPUR HOUSE

Dear Friend,

You ~~HAVE TO COME HELP US~~ are cordially invited to a house ~~THAT WANTS TO SCARE YOU~~ unlike any you've ever entered——one that understands your wishes and dreams, and wants to ~~KEEP YOU FOREVER~~ help make them come true.

Few have been called ~~AND EVEN FEWER ESCAPE,~~ but if you're reading this, you're one of the Special ones. Come. Let's play.

Most sincerely,

~~Larkspur~~ *SHADOW HOUSE*

Enter Shadow House . . . if you dare.

1. Get the FREE Shadow House app for your phone or tablet.
2. Each image in the book reveals a ghost story in the app.
3. Step into ghost stories, where the choices you make determine your fate.

 For tablet or phone.

scholastic.com/shadowhouse

No Way Out

DAN POBLOCKI

SCHOLASTIC INC.

Library of Congress Control Number Available

ISBN 978-0-545-92552-5

10 9 8 7 6 5 4 3 2 1   17 18 19 20 21

First edition, September 2017

Printed in Heshan, China   62

Scholastic US: 557 Broadway • New York, NY 10012
Scholastic Canada: 604 King Street West • Toronto, ON M5V 1E1
Scholastic New Zealand Limited: Private Bag 94407 • Greenmount, Manukau 2141
Scholastic UK Ltd.: Euston House • 24 Eversholt Street • London NW1 1DB

For Erin Black, who is a wonderful editor
and much spookier than she admits

CHAPTER 1

ON THE EDGE of the starlit meadow, Azumi's thoughts throbbed in her head in time with her footsteps. *My fault Marcus is dead. My fault Moriko's gone. My fault we trusted the monster, my fault, my fault, my fault my fault my fault—*

Something snagged Azumi's sneaker, and she tripped forward, the tall grass padding her fall.

Poppy and Dash continued on, unaware that Azumi was sprawled behind them. They marched quickly and quietly, parallel to the dark woods several yards to their right.

Wait! Please—

She tried to call out, but her voice was stuck in her throat. Would calling them even help? Everything here was out to destroy them. What was the point?

My fault—

Larkspur House glared down at her from atop the hill to her left, and Azumi shuddered. Something inside its dark windows wished to keep her there forever. If the hallways could change shape, the wallpaper turn into toxic tendrils, and the greenhouse contain acres of forest, what was stopping Larkspur from catapulting its bricks and glass and metal spikes far into the meadow and pounding her flat?

No. She had to concentrate. She had to stick to the plan, do what Poppy and Dash said.

They were even farther away now—focused and determined to make it quickly back to the driveway and the safety of Hardscrabble Road. Dash limped a little, and Poppy tended to him every few steps. So why hadn't she noticed that Azumi wasn't with them?

Azumi pressed her lips together and was about to stand when something rustled the grass by her feet. Turning back, she noticed the shadow of the thing that had tripped her only a few inches away. Instinct made her scramble aside. But when the breeze rustled the grass, showing Azumi what looked like matted and faded-blue hair glistening in the starlight, panic whooshed into her head like a harsh gust of wind, and she froze, wide-eyed, her chest heaving.

Blue hair . . .

Moriko? she tried to say, but her voice wouldn't come past her lips.

You can't be . . . You're dead . . .

This . . . isn't . . . real.

A trick . . . Just like how the creature dressed as you, like a costume . . .

She forced herself to her feet. From up the hill, Larkspur House loomed. Azumi could feel it grinning at her—another version of that same creature that had pretended to be her sister.

But the house is only a costume too . . . , she thought.

Wood and brick and stone and . . . blood . . .

Azumi shook her head violently, scattering the cobwebs of anxiety that her brain kept constructing around her thoughts. She steeled herself, pushing her fear to the edges of her imagination, then peered at the dark mass that was hidden by the long grass.

It's happening again . . .

You're not really here . . .

Wake up, Azumi . . . Wake up . . . !

A harsh breeze parted the grass, finally revealing the thing that Azumi had tripped over. Her eyes grew wide with horror. It was a body. Pieces of dirty clothing formed the shape of a torso, arms, legs. She knew these clothes. It was Moriko!

Not again . . . please! I don't want to see . . .

The wind caught several pieces of blue hair and lifted them from her sister's withered skull. They rose up like gossamer strands before rushing forward and clinging to Azumi's face. Her vision swirled as she screamed, her voice shattering the quiet night. As she inhaled, the hairs seemed to creep into her throat and up her nostrils, choking her. She scratched at her face, grabbing at the sharp strands, but she was blinded by a stinging sensation in her eyes. She could hear something scrabbling through the grass near her feet, and she imagined her sister's fingers clawing their way toward her ankle, while somewhere in the woods the monster heard her and came rushing back to finish its job.

Hands clasped her shoulders and spun her around. She was too shocked to cry out.

Poppy was standing behind her, Dash at her side. "Azumi! What's wrong?"

Azumi blinked, still gagging, but all of a sudden her face was clear, the hair gone. Carefully, she licked at her lips. The blue hair had only been another trick—the house, the shadow creature was still playing with her. Or maybe it was her own mind . . .

Azumi leapt forward and threw her arms around Poppy, pulling her away from the spot where her sister's body lay. "It's M-Moriko," Azumi sputtered. "She's come back." But when she pointed toward the grass, there was no body. Instead, she saw that the thing she'd tripped over was merely a long tree branch, bleached by the sun.

Her skin flashed cold.

"This branch wasn't here," said Azumi. "It was my sister. She grabbed at my foot. I swear! She wanted to kill me—"

"It wasn't real," said Poppy.

"Shh," said Dash. "Keep your voices down." He glanced over Azumi's shoulder toward the edge of woods. Marcus was back there somewhere, lying beneath the tree where the creature had tossed him. "It could be following us."

"I'm . . . I'm sorry . . ." Azumi covered her face, hiding tears. "It scared me."

"I'm sure it did." Poppy sighed. "But it was fake." She rubbed Azumi's back. "We've got to stay strong. Don't let the house in your head."

"Too late for that," said Azumi. "I don't know how to get it *out* of my head."

"From now on," said Dash, "we have to keep closer together. If anyone trips and falls, or even just sees something weird, let everyone know. Immediately. We can't let the house separate us."

"Okay," said Azumi, wiping at her nose.

Poppy stared into the woods, listening. "If it was still coming for us, we'd hear it, wouldn't we? Crunching through the brush?"

"Unless it's changed shape again," said Dash, "and now it looks like *someone else*."

Azumi's skin prickled as the three glanced at one another, suddenly suspicious.

But she could trust them, couldn't she? They'd been out of her sight for only a second. Not enough time for anything to—

"Let me see your eyes," said Poppy, stepping in front of her.

"Me?" Azumi's cheeks tingled with hurt. She scowled, then widened her eyes at the other girl. "*Brown*. Not gold."

A howling cry rose up from the darkness back near where Marcus had fallen. Azumi slumped her shoulders, trying to shrink down inside herself. Poppy clasped Azumi's hand, and Dash stepped closer. Their warmth erased some of Azumi's chill, and she felt grateful—that they trusted her, even after she'd fought them so hard about Moriko; that they understood her fear; that she wasn't alone.

But you are *alone . . .*

Azumi squeezed her eyes shut again.

The howl echoed across the grounds, and then died away. The silence that followed was even more frightening. There was no way to tell where the monster was now.

"Come on," said Dash, tugging at the girls' arms. "We've got a long way to go around the house before we reach the driveway. And I don't think that thing is giving up anytime soon."

"Neither are we," said Poppy, unable to control the quaver in her voice.

CHAPTER 2

THEY MOVED QUICKLY, almost at a run. They needed to get away from the spot where Azumi had screamed. If the creature had heard her, it would know exactly where they were, as if they'd stuck a pin in a map. They formed a tight line, keeping one another in sight. Dash wondered if it was foolish to think that they could even try to hide. If this entire estate was a thinking, scheming being, what were the chances that it didn't know exactly where they were? Maybe the house was still toying with them, giving them a little bit of hope—*Run! Go! Escape!*—so it could continue to feed off their fear. Wasn't that how it worked?

The silvery grass ahead began to lose its luster. Dash glanced up and noticed that heavy clouds were closing in, blocking the starlight. Now they'd have to stay closer to the woods, or else risk becoming lost in the gathering darkness. But getting closer to the trees might put them closer to the shadow creature, or the Specials and Dylan.

As he rushed through the darkening field, Dash shuddered, thinking of the clown mask Dylan had been wearing. The warm plastic had moved, as if it was part of Dylan, as if he belonged to the house now.

It was only one of the reasons he'd decided to leave his brother behind.

The house was controlling his brother—like a plant whose roots had twined around another's. But Dylan was different from the angry ghosts of the orphans who'd once lived here. Dash was sure of it. Poppy had solved the puzzle of how to free the others from the house. When they'd given Randolph a harmonica and Esme her notebook, they'd remembered themselves and faded away, released from the house's grasp. Even Cyrus's withered old ghost had found freedom when Poppy had handed him his old journal.

But Poppy had no ideas for freeing Dylan. Cyrus had never taken anything from him that Dash could return. So what did Dylan need in order to be released?

Dash forced the thought from his head. Dylan was already

gone. As awful as it was to imagine, Dash knew that he'd have to leave his brother behind and get as far away from Larkspur as his feet would take him.

Azumi grabbed at Dash's shoulder as she stared into the distance ahead.

"Why are we stopping?" asked Poppy. "What's wrong?"

"Do you guys see that?" Azumi nodded at the darkness. "Or is the house messing with my head again?"

"See what?" asked Dash. But then he noticed dim silhouettes of shacks or tents throughout the wide meadow about a hundred feet away. Under the cloudy sky, it was impossible to make out any details. "Whoa. What *is* all this?"

"Look!" Poppy whispered as they drifted closer, pointing at one of the taller shapes. "Is that a . . . a Ferris wheel?"

"It's a carnival," said Azumi. "Like the one that comes through my town every fall, right around when school starts. I think I see a carousel."

"And a fun house," said Poppy, her voice wavering as she pointed. "I went into one of those in the city once with the other girls from my group home. They tried to scare me in the mirror maze, but my Girl . . . Connie . . . she showed me where to hide from them."

"And Larkspur is trying to scare *us* again," said Dash, clipping the discussion short. "Come on, let's go around."

"We'll have to either go close to the house or into the woods for a bit," said Azumi. "Neither seems like a very good idea."

"Wouldn't it be safer to just go straight through?" asked Poppy. "It looks deserted."

"Do you really want to trust what it *looks* like?" asked Dash.

Poppy hugged her chest. "So then, what? Turn around and go the way we came? Head around the other side of the house? What about the . . . the thing? The creature?"

Sounds of breaking branches and crunching brush echoed out of the woods behind them. Then came a low growling noise. The three grabbed hands and huddled together.

"There's no other way," said Azumi, shivering as she glanced back at the dim shapes that made up the makeshift carnival. "We've got to go through."

Dash sighed. "But we know it's a trick."

"We've managed to get past the house's other tricks," Poppy said, sounding much more confident than Dash felt.

The image of Marcus came to him, humming his uncle's tune while bravely confronting the creature back at the edge of the forest. "Not all of us," he whispered.

But Poppy squeezed his hand and Azumi's and then began to march forward, pulling everyone along with her.

CHAPTER 3

SCREAMING BROKE THE SILENCE.

The three stopped, wide-eyed.

But then the screaming turned to laughter. In the field ahead, it sounded like children were playing inside the dark carnival. The clouds overhead grew thicker, darkening the meadow.

As they approached the boxy silhouettes, the laughs and screams of children stopped abruptly, and all they could hear was the shush of the wind through the grass. Poppy paused for a second, shivering at the sudden silence, then squared her shoulders and moved ahead. At last, she could make out some details. Most of the tents and booths were small, with pitched roofs and striped canvas walls. They made Poppy think of a jail cell or a cage at a zoo. She edged cautiously past the first booth, peering into the shadows. Beyond the canvas flaps was a dusty wooden table and a weather-worn chair. A ticket booth.

"This place reminds me of something I found in the class-room back inside Larkspur," said Poppy. "One of the *first* orphans had drawn a picture of a carnival, with a Ferris wheel and rides and balloons."

"So this might all just be a memory," said Azumi. "Like . . . come to life."

"The house's memory?" asked Dash.

"Or one of the orphans'. Maybe Cyrus brought in a carnival for them once, before things turned bad."

"And he just left it here to rot?"

"Well, no," said Azumi. "But we know that Larkspur burned down, yet . . . *there it stands*." She pointed up the hill to where the mansion remained—defiant and dark. "So if the house can rebuild *itself*, maybe it can also rebuild other things that once existed here."

"If you're both so determined to go through," said Dash, stepping forward, "can we at least do it quickly?"

"It's our best option, Dash," said Poppy, following him closely and feeling strangely embarrassed. He had never totally dis-agreed with her before. "Besides, not every ghost we've met in the house has been bad. What if the first orphans are trying to help us right now? To give us a clue, or a tool, to find our way home?"

13

"But we already know the way home," said Dash. "We get to the driveway. We find the gate. We leave!"

"I actually agree with Dash," said Azumi. "It does seem like it's supposed to slow us down."

Now *Azumi* was against Poppy too?

"And that's exactly what it's doing." Dash nodded. "This carnival is giving whatever might be following us—the Specials, the shadow creature, and who knows what else—time to catch up."

Poppy pressed her lips together and dug her fingernails into her palms.

Azumi reached out and yanked everyone to a stop. "Wait, what's that?" Ahead, the tents appeared to have grown taller, the stripes on their canvases stretched longer and slimmer like gaps between giant teeth.

"What do you see?" Poppy asked. She was worried about Azumi. She'd been mumbling to herself. Twitching, the way Marcus had when he'd been hearing music from his uncle. When he'd been lying to them.

Could they trust her anymore?

But Poppy knew what it felt like to be called crazy, to have no one believe her. At Thursday's Hope, the other young residents had teased her for believing that a mysterious girl had always watched her from inside mirrors. It was only that

14

morning at Larkspur that she discovered who the girl really was: her cousin. Consolida Caldwell. She'd tried to warn Poppy about Larkspur, but Poppy hadn't understood until it was too late, and she was trapped inside.

She was so close to escaping now. If only Azumi and Dash would focus, they might help discover some weakness in the house's armor.

"There's a row of people," whispered Azumi, pointing as she stepped backward. "Standing there in the dark."

Poppy squinted, but all she could make out were the tents' stripes along the midway corridor which curved to the left, heading back up toward the house. "Do *you* see anyone, Dash?" Poppy asked.

"I'm not making it up!" said Azumi. "They're right there! Along the tents on the right. Five of them."

Dash shushed her, and Poppy saw Azumi flinch. "Maybe we *should* turn around and go back the other way," he whispered.

Poppy took a few more steps into the murk before she could see them too—hulking, dark shapes all in a row. "Dash, can I use your flashlight for just a moment?"

"I don't know how much battery I have left."

"Can you check?"

With a huff, Dash pulled the phone from his pocket. Its glow lit his face from below. His eyes widened. "One hundred percent? How?" He shuddered and then turned on the flashlight app. The pale light revealed only several feet of the path ahead of them. In order to see through the darkness, Poppy would have to get closer.

"I'm scared," said Azumi, shrinking farther back.

"Trust me," said Poppy confidently, adjusting her messenger bag across her shoulder before grabbing for Azumi's chilled hand. The others knew that Poppy's instincts had already saved them several times. Why should Poppy stop now?

Dash scrambled to keep up as the girls quickly passed him by. "This doesn't feel right, Poppy. Can I please have my phone back?"

But Poppy pretended she hadn't heard him.

A few more steps forward and the shapes on the right side of the midway were suddenly clear. They weren't people. Not exactly.

They were clowns.

To Poppy's relief, she realized quickly that they were not *actual* clowns, but plaster statues standing in a sharp row. Most of them were over five feet tall, and some looked older than others. One had three multicolored spikes of hair poking up from his bone-white skull; his triangular, rose-colored nose squashed almost flat; a crooked smile revealing straight but yellowing teeth. He wore a pale jumpsuit marked with tiny red and blue dots, and his hand was raised in a frozen wave. Another had a small, more oval-shaped head, a huge bulbous nose, and hair made of straw, with eyes that were crossed out by haphazard smears of blue paint. His maniacal grin took up the entire bottom half of his face, stretching from one ear to the other and all the way down to his chin. One frowning bald figure stood out to Poppy. He wore a jumpsuit covered in an indigo diamond pattern, and he seemed to be staring directly into Poppy's eyes.

"Uh-uh," said Dash, crossing his arms and keeping his distance. "No way. This gets a big NOPE from me."

"But it's the only way," said Poppy.

"I'm not walking by them either," said Azumi.

The clowns stared blankly out across the path, as if they meant to entertain an immense crowd that no longer existed in this abandoned place.

"Poppy," whispered Dash, an edge to his voice. "Where are you going?"

Poppy froze. She hadn't even realized that she'd moved toward the tent opposite the row of clowns. There was a seam in the canvas that appeared to be torn.

Dash stood several feet in front of the row of plaster figurines, while Azumi hunched beside him, entranced by the clown with the frowning face.

"I . . . I don't know," said Poppy, her cheeks burning. Hadn't they just agreed to stay closer together? "I think I found a new route."

"Uh, no," said Dash. "We should turn back. Find another way around."

Poppy pulled at the seam, making the gap wider, and then shone the light inside. Musty shadows yawned from within. A wide sign hung over the closed flaps on the right—the word GAMES had been painted in an old-fashioned font, and illustrations of laughing children with grotesque smiles bookended each side.

"Hello?" she whispered, looking around for anyone who might be hiding inside.

Dash scoffed. "You really think someone will answer you?"

Sensing that they were getting ready to bolt, Poppy took Azumi by the elbow and led her to the gap in the games tent. Quickly, she tore the seam open. "*Here's* our way around," she said, nudging Azumi through the new slit in the wall.

"Poppy!" Dash said in shock. "No!"

"She's fine," said Poppy. "Right, Azumi?"

From inside the gap, Azumi called out a nervous answer. "I'm . . . I'm okay. The tent's filled with carnival games. We can go through here and pass the creepy clowns outside."

Dash joined the girls at the tear in the canvas. He gritted his teeth. "I want to let it be known that I am totally against this plan."

"Would I lead you astray?" asked Poppy, forcing a smile as she stepped carefully through the canvas.

Once inside, Dash took his phone from her. The three crept across the space.

The light illuminated rows of stuffed animals hanging on the wall behind a barrier made of rusted chicken wire. Prizes.

"Which way?" he asked, his voice quieter now.

The eyes of the stuffed animals stared back at them.

Poppy nodded at a sign hanging from the center of the cage—bold black letters had been hand-painted on a large white square. "That looks familiar."

"Oh, no," whispered Azumi with a shudder, clinging to Poppy's arm.

Slowly, Dash read the sign aloud. "*Let's . . . play?* Last time something in the house asked us to *play*, the Specials showed up and tried to kill us."

"All we have to do is get across the tent," said Poppy. "Find another seam. Tear it open."

Dash sighed, shaking his head.

CHAPTER 4

AS POPPY LED everyone forward, Azumi looked back at the slit in the canvas they'd come through.

She didn't know who to trust anymore, and couldn't stop the flood of questions—*Is Poppy right? Do we go this way? Can we believe our eyes?*—from racing through her thoughts over and over until she was dizzy. Maybe that was why she was so exhausted, why she wished to just lie down and go to sleep, instead of walking, *sleep*walking through these infinite nightmares.

Get it together, Azumi told herself, shaking her head. *You cannot let Dash and Poppy see you like this or they'll leave you here just like they left poor Dylan with his sad clown mask.* How could they not have noticed that he'd been hiding inside that plaster figurine out on the midway?

Then she wondered, *Why didn't I tell them?*

Azumi glanced back at the hole in the canvas.

The frowning clown was peering through the gap.

Azumi shrieked and then tripped over her own feet, falling to the ground. Poppy and Dash rushed to help her back up.

"What's wrong?" barked Dash.

"Did you see something?" Poppy asked.

But when Azumi glanced back, the opening was dark. There were no clowns there. Only shadows.

"I . . . I thought I did," said Azumi. "But it was nothing. Just jumpy, I guess."

Dash and Poppy watched her for a few seconds before they turned toward the games and the prizes that surrounded them in this new tent.

Why am I the only one being tormented like this? Azumi wondered. Poppy and Dash were practically fine. An ember of anger sparked in her belly, jealousy that they weren't feeling what she was feeling or seeing what she was seeing. It hurt that she was alone in this bubble of confusion.

But you're more normal than they are, she told herself. *You've always been normal. And smart.* Weren't those *good* things? Azumi thought of all the activities she used to do in her old school outside of Seattle—playing forward on the soccer team, leading her die-hard study group, being the student government representative for her grade. And when she'd needed to protect herself from her own mind, from her nightly dreams of walking through the suicide forest in Japan, she'd gone as far as seeking a boarding school across the entire country.

Who but a very brave girl would do such a thing? Neither of *them*, that was for sure.

When they were about halfway across the dark space, the tent trembled.

There was a sound of fabric shuffling, followed by a great, loud *whush!* Azumi looked back at where they'd entered and yelped. The entry had disappeared.

Dash felt the earth tilt as dizziness crept inside his skull. He focused on Poppy to straighten himself out.

"What did you do?" he shouted.

Her brow wrinkled. But then she walked over to the spot where the gap had closed. "It's only canvas," said Poppy, tugging at the seam. "We can just open it—" But she couldn't. The opening seemed to have been sealed over. She scraped her nails against the fabric, and after a few seconds, Poppy glanced sheepishly over her shoulder. "It's not working."

"But *it's only canvas*," Dash echoed, flinching at the venom in his voice. He blinked and cleared his throat, trying to find a seed of calm somewhere in the whirlwind of his brain. "Can you lift it from the bottom? We'll crawl underneath."

Poppy bent down and tried to get a grip, but now the canvas was attached to the ground itself. Dash rushed over and grappled with the tent, but he couldn't get it to budge either. In a fit of fury, he kicked and thrashed against the wall, as if his anger could break through to the midway, until he fell away, winded and faint.

"Dash, are you all right?" asked Poppy, reaching for his shoulder, but he flailed away from her. She shrank back, biting her lip.

He was fighting with everything he had to keep from bursting into angry tears. After everything they'd been through in the past few hours—Moriko's transformation into the creature, Marcus's death, Dash's decision to walk away from his brother's tormented ghost—it was a horror to imagine that he'd lose it over something as simple as a carnival tent. But then nothing here was simple. "I told you this was a trick!" he yelled.

Poppy closed her eyes, as if he'd just lobbed a water balloon at her and she was resigned that it would smack her in the face.

When would they all stop being so naive? he fumed. What would it take? Another of them *dying*?

"Can't we cut it open?" asked Azumi.

"With what?"

"Smash one of the lightbulbs. Use the jagged edge."

"This glass is paper-thin. It'll never—"

The strings of lightbulbs hanging overhead were suddenly all aglow, illuminating the game stations inside the dim room.

"What's it doing?" asked Azumi.

Poppy rushed over to the cage with the stuffed animals, snatching the sign from the chicken wire. "*Let's play*," she read pointedly.

"You've got to be crazy!" Dash yelled, following her.

"Don't call me that!" said Poppy, scowling. She turned and headed toward the ring-toss table.

"I'm sorry. But you're not the only one trapped in here, Poppy. *Our* lives are at stake too. The way out is closed off now because of you. What if something worse happens?"

Poppy's face flushed red. "We can't just do *nothing*!"

"Let's search for another way out," Dash said. "Another seam we can rip open."

"Fine. Let's look."

The group explored the tent's perimeter, but there was no other way out.

Dash threw his hands up. "We could have turned back! Ignored the tents altogether. We could have found another way to the driveway."

"I'm sorry!" Poppy cried out. "You're right. We could've gone into the woods! But would that have been any better than this?"

"Yes!"

Azumi backed away from both of them.

Poppy picked up the sign again. "I believe this will work. We have to at least try."

"Or it might make something else happen," Dash said. "Something worse."

CHAPTER 5

"LOOK AT THEM all." Poppy stood in front of the partition made of twisted wire, her fingers looped through the small holes. The canvas wall across from her was covered in little stuffed animals—tigers, frogs, bears, and more—and their black plastic eyes shone in the beam of Dash's flashlight. "They're almost beautiful, all together like this." She rattled the cage lightly, but it wouldn't budge.

"If we're going to play," said Dash, "what do you hope to win?"

Poppy sighed and then backed away, giving him a sidelong glance.

"What about the rabbit, the bear, and the cat?" asked Azumi.

"What are you talking about?" Poppy asked.

"Azumi's right," said Dash, pointing beyond the chicken wire at several of the stuffed animals. "Look. Up there. A rabbit. And on the bottom right. A bear. And over on the left. A cat. They look just like the Specials."

Well, not just *like the Specials*, thought Azumi. These were toys—much smaller than the ghosts that had been chasing them through Larkspur. Now they were huggable-size and plush, like her own stuffed animals that her mother had donated to charity a couple of years prior.

She didn't mention the raggedy clown hanging right in the middle. It looked like the one that had been staring at her through the gap in the tent.

"Azumi!" Poppy said, flinging her arms around the other girl's neck. Azumi made a surprised peeping sound. "You're brilliant."

Azumi smiled, satisfied that she was still useful to them, happy that she was able to hide her fear behind a mask.

"It's an ambush!" Dash exclaimed.

"It's not an ambush if we're prepared," said Poppy, her voice steady and loud. She stepped back and stared at the cage. "I have the things that Cyrus took from them: the doll, the football, and the candy. Now how are we going to get to them? This wall seems pretty solid."

Dash examined the sides of the barrier, where heavy bolts met vertical metal gutters. "It looks like this whole panel should slide up." He yanked on it, trying to force it to open, then yelped and let go. Blood beaded where the wire had caught him. "Ow." He held his hands to his T-shirt, leaving red marks.

"You okay?" asked Poppy.

"I'll be fine, but this stupid thing—"

"I think we've got to win a prize," said Azumi, trying to find the same confidence in her tone that Poppy had used seconds earlier. "Isn't that how carnival games work?"

"I'm pretty good at the ring toss," said Poppy. "Let's start there."

"Let's get this over with," said Dash.

Azumi followed the others over to the table with the bottles. As Poppy reached for a trio of silver rings on the counter nearby, Azumi stared at the miniature version of the frowning clown. "Good luck," she said.

CHAPTER 6

DASH STOOD BESIDE Poppy with his arms crossed. "How's this going to work?" he asked, trying to not sound annoyed. He knew he should be sending Poppy good vibes, yet he couldn't stop thinking that playing these games was a mistake, even if there *were* animals that looked like the Specials locked behind the chicken-wire cage. The pain in Dash's leg had finally begun to lessen; he barely even needed his crutch anymore. Their group should be moving along as fast as they could.

But then Poppy flicked her wrist, releasing one of the rings. It sailed a short distance toward the platform with the bottles and landed around one of the glass necks. Poppy and Azumi cheered. A bell rang, and from the rear wall, there came a scraping noise.

Dash turned to find that a dangling string of lightbulbs was flashing above the rows of animals. But more important, the chicken-wire barrier had raised about three inches.

"Whoa," said Poppy.

"If Poppy keeps winning, that cage will open all the way," said Azumi. "Then we can grab the animals."

Dash sighed. He couldn't shake the feeling that this room, the game, and the prizes might all be a trick. Larkspur knew what was in their heads, and it was probably anticipating their next moves. He wished he could just smash through the barrier without thinking and tear the dolls into pieces.

Poppy threw out the next ring. For a moment, it seemed to hover over one of the bottle's necks, ready to drop for another success. But then it wobbled and came down askew, just missing the target.

The mesh cage slammed down again, making them jump.

"Shoot," Poppy whispered. "I have to start over."

"Great!" said Dash, squinting at her. "Take all the time you need."

"I'm pretty good at Skee-Ball," said Azumi. She strolled over to the row of machines, palming one of the balls, feeling its weight.

Poppy lowered her voice, smoothing out the rough edges. "What about you, Dash? Any games you want to try?"

"I don't want to do any of this," Dash said, rolling his eyes. Why did she look like she was having fun?

He glanced around the space. Another stand caught his eye. The sign above it flashed with tiny lights. *Carnival Punks! Knock 'Em Down!* Three shelves were crowded with colorful little creatures made out of beanbags, each with an exaggerated, comically monstrous face and wild wool hair. Several balls were stacked on the counter. Nearby, a little sign read: *See how many you can hit in a row!*

Before Dash could pick up one of the balls, he heard the jingle of another little bell. Poppy whooped. The ring she'd just tossed was still swinging around the bottle's neck. The chicken-wire cage rattled as it rose up several inches again.

"Nice!" said Azumi.

Dash was just about to force himself to congratulate Poppy when something hit the wall of the tent behind him. Dash jumped away, but the canvas continued to bounce and shudder. Poppy and Azumi watched, their mouths open in terror.

Someone outside was trying to get in.

CHAPTER 7

POPPY STEELED HER nerves, blocking out the rattling canvas. She rushed over to Dash. He flinched when she touched his shoulder. "If we're trapped in here," she said calmly, "whoever or whatever it is must be stuck out there." Dash raised his head, eyes wide. She nodded at the booths they'd each picked. "We know that if we keep winning at these games, the prize cage will open and we'll set the Specials free." Nodding at the canvas wall, she added, "*That* is just a distraction to stop us. Ignore it. Let's do this."

Dash returned to the carnival punks and Azumi lunged toward the Skee-Ball machines. Poppy gathered up several rings from the counter. She concentrated as she pulled her wrist back, but then Azumi screamed and a buzzer rang out, and the chicken-wire barrier came crashing back down again.

"Gutter ball," Azumi called out after a moment, shivering.

"Block out everything else," said Poppy. "Just be here." She tapped her temple. "Inside your own head."

She watched as Azumi snatched another ball, closed her eyes, and took a deep breath. Then, whipping her arm forward, she rolled the ball up the alley. At the end, it flew in a perfect arc and landed directly in the top hole, the one worth fifty points.

Lights flashed around the tent and the barrier slid open— wider this time, but still not wide enough for anyone to reach through and take any of the animals. Then Poppy noticed something strange. The rabbit, the bear, and the cat all seemed to have grown a little. Her stomach dropped as she understood: Poppy, Dash, and Azumi weren't the only ones playing games here. Of course the house had set this up. She couldn't let the others know. It would only throw them off.

Dash yelped as he knocked over several of the carnival punks. Poppy watched the cage jolt upward a few more inches. And at the same time, the three animals that mattered grew even larger, like balloons about to pop. Poppy ran to the rear wall, grabbing at her messenger bag and flipping it open. She dug around inside and removed the flattened football, several pieces of candy, and the headless doll.

"What are you doing, Poppy?" asked Dash.

"Getting ready. Keep going. Don't miss!"

The thing outside the tent began to move around the walls, battering at the thick canvas. But Azumi closed her eyes again and flung another ball up the Skee-Ball alley.

Ding! Ding! Ding!

Another bull's-eye!

"Good job, Azumi!" Poppy called out.

The cage shifted a few more inches upward and the rabbit, bear, and cat swelled further—their weight pulling on the cords they were hanging from, jouncing the other stuffed animals so the entire wall of prizes was suddenly frenzied, as if it were alive. Poppy braced herself. She realized that if the barrier opened at the same time the Specials grew to their full size, the three might come through at once, and she couldn't take them all on by herself.

Azumi seemed to be doing well enough, so Poppy called out to Dash, "Would you help me out?" He rushed over, and she handed him the deflated football. "We need to be ready," she said, and he nodded. "Azumi, keep it up!"

Azumi groaned and then let another Skee-Ball fly. It bounced on the edge of the ring and Poppy felt her rib cage tighten—but it hit the target. There was another blast of bells and flash of lights, and the cage opened wider.

The cords holding the animals squealed as the Specials started to burst at their seams. Poppy tried to reach for the cat, which was closest. Her fingers brushed against the dangling plush feet, but she couldn't grab hold. "Poppy, be careful!" shouted Dash.

There came a loud whomping sound as whatever was drumming on the tent began to attack the spot behind the wall of prizes. The stuffed animals jittered and shook. Suddenly, from the upper left corner, the rabbit fell to the ground. Wide-eyed, Poppy stuck her head through the gap and bent over the counter. She grasped the stuffed animal and yanked it up as Dash pulled her back out of the booth. It took a second before Poppy realized what—or *who*—she was holding in her hands. Aloysius. The orphan who hadn't been able to speak. Who had loved candy until Cyrus had started giving him sweets that had made him sick.

The rabbit was heavy, and he slipped quickly through her fingers and landed at her feet with a thump. The strings of light flickered overhead, making the rabbit thing appear to squirm. Or maybe he really *was* squirming . . .

"Azumi, wait!" Dash cried out, but it was too late. She rolled another bull's-eye and the cage opened all the way. The cat and the bear also dropped from their cords, falling behind the counter.

Poppy didn't hesitate. She bent down and clutched at the stuffed rabbit's head, digging her fingers into his stitching.

She shoved away thoughts of real skin and bones as she wrenched the fabric apart, revealing the plastic rabbit mask that was hidden inside the stuffing.

The pounding behind the wall of prizes grew louder and a scraping noise began, as if whatever was out there was now trying to tear its way in.

Poppy yanked the rabbit mask away, tossing it into the shadows near the edge of the tent. A pale face appeared and stared up at her in surprise from within the cushioned white head. The boy's eyes grew wide and his jaw dropped open, the dark stain around his mouth and neck fading as he caught his breath. "Aloysius," said Poppy, tears welling in her own eyes. "You're going to be okay. We're here to save you."

Dash and Azumi were each bent over one of the other Specials. Dash grabbed at the bear mask and Azumi took the cat, and soon Irving and Matilda were revealed, wearing shocked expressions, their eyes pooling with relief and fear.

The boy by Poppy leaned forward, struggling to sit up inside the cocoon of stuffed animal. She held his shoulders as he stretched out his limbs and then burst through the rest of the stitching. The costume tore away with a satisfying ripping sound and revealed his gray-and-white Larkspur uniform. He opened his mouth as if to say *thank you* or *hurry* or *watch out*— but nothing came.

Poppy trembled, remembering the candies she'd meant to give him. She retrieved them quickly from the counter by her shoulder. Their cellophane wrappers crinkled in her palm. "These candies are what Cyrus stole from you," she explained. "Take them so you can leave this place."

Dash helped Irving out of the bear trappings, the chains around Irving's ankles rattling like the musical chimes that had come from the prize booths. He handed the boy the deflated football. Matilda stood up, clutching the doll that Azumi passed to her; then she turned her piercing blue eyes toward Poppy.

The scratching outside the tent went on. The other stuffed animals continued to shake and dance. Several of them tumbled to the ground.

Aloysius stared at the candies in his hand. "Go on," said Poppy, nodding encouragement. "Try them." She suddenly remembered Ms. Tate telling her *Never take candy from strangers*, and she felt her face flush with embarrassment. He quickly unwrapped one of them. The hard little black nugget looked like the plastic eyes of the stuffed animals on the tent's wall. Aloysius closed his own eyes and popped it into his mouth, and, with some difficulty, swallowed it down. They waited.

Poppy took a step back. Something was wrong.

The tent had gone quiet. The scratching at the canvas had stopped.

Then, with a loud belch, black liquid spouted from Aloysius's lips and leaked from his nose. He opened his mouth as if trying to speak. "*Agghhh*," he moaned, doubling over in pain, the poisonous goo dribbling onto the ground.

Poppy glanced over at Dash and Azumi, who were standing with Irving and Matilda. Neither of the other Specials was reacting in the way she expected them to. When they'd given Randolph and Esme the items that had set them free—the harmonica and the notebook—the effect had taken place almost immediately. They'd smiled—looking as if they'd rediscovered a former best friend—and then disintegrated into a sweet and peaceful nothingness. Irving and Matilda stared at her, brows furrowed, looking as confused as Poppy felt.

"Why isn't it working?" asked Azumi.

"Where did you get these objects?" whispered Matilda, her voice buzzing.

"They were in a filing cabinet in Cyrus's tower," said Dash. "They're yours, aren't they?"

Hearing Cyrus's name, Irving dropped the football.

"These aren't ours anymore," Matilda said. "They're his now."

Aloysius retched, shivering as he hunched over, and Poppy cringed, guilt gurgling in her stomach. She reached out to rub his back, but he flinched from her touch. "I'm sorry," she whispered, glancing around the frightened group. There was little difference between any of them. Everyone was terrified. "I messed up."

"It's happening again," said Matilda, touching her own face.

Aloysius stood up, black tears now streaking his cheeks. He pointed at his mouth and moaned again. "It's my fault," Poppy whimpered. She wanted to grab him and give him a hug, but she knew that in only a few moments, his mask would begin to grow back and he'd not be so innocent anymore.

All of a sudden, the wall behind the prizes trembled. An earsplitting sound echoed through the tent as the canvas tore open and the rest of the stuffed animals tumbled to the ground. Two flaps swung back, revealing a shadowy tunnel of stripes that led back up the hill toward Larkspur House.

CHAPTER 8

OUTSIDE, LIGHTNING FLASHED and thunder
rumbled. The house's roofline lit up, all spikes and spires.

"Is someone out there?" Azumi asked. Dash shushed her.

Poppy moved closer to them. To her surprise, the Specials
followed, seeming to tremble as they too stared out into the
darkness.

"It's the house," Dash whispered. "It wants us to go back."

"No," said Azumi. "Larkspur can't make me do *anything*
anymore. I won't let it!"

Poppy sniffled. "We've got something more important to
deal with right now."

Dash widened his eyes. "More important than getting
away from the house again?"

"Or figuring out what's out there?" asked Azumi. "Something tore open the tent."

Aloysius groaned again, more black goo running from his mouth.

Then Dash and Azumi realized what Poppy meant. If they didn't figure out how to release the Specials, their enemy would be back—closer than before.

Poppy couldn't let that happen. "We're going to help them," she said, reaching into her messenger bag again. Her fingers closed upon a small, crinkly object she'd forgotten was in there. She opened her hand, showing Aloysius the last cherry cough drop she'd brought with her from the city. His eyes grew large. Poppy wasn't sure if it was because he was surprised, or if maybe the rabbit mask was transforming his features again.

"It's not candy *exactly*," said Poppy, "but it's sweet. Cyrus never touched it. It might make you feel better."

Tentatively, Aloysius took the drop and unwrapped it. He glanced nervously at Matilda and Irving, as if for permission, but they were distracted, writhing in pain. Aloysius popped it into his mouth and his face immediately changed. Dimples creased into his cheeks as his smile grew. He opened his mouth, and this time, the only thing that spilled out was laughter. A soft breeze blew through the tent, and then the boy was gone.

"It worked!" Poppy cried out. Matilda and Irving pulled

themselves away from their torment, hugging each other tightly. Poppy realized how horrible it must be for them to see one another suffer, unable to do anything about it throughout decades as captives of Larkspur.

"What else do you have in that bag, Poppy?" Azumi asked.

Before Poppy could answer, another streak of lightning spread in a ragged arc across the sky. Several yards up the path, five figures lit up. The plaster clowns. The one in the center stepped into the glow from the lights hanging in the games tent. Its dark, frowning lips immediately stood out against its pale face.

Azumi shuddered and then tripped backward into Poppy's arms. "I'm not crazy," she murmured, as if to herself.

"Dylan!" Dash shouted. "Is that you?"

The clown threw its head back and chortled. It then tore away its indigo costume and Dylan's red-and-black plaid shirt appeared underneath, along with his shorts and sandals. His features transitioned—the red from his clown mask blooming like wounds on his nose and mouth.

"He was watching us the whole time?" asked Azumi. "Beating on the tent like that?"

"Trying to scare us." Dash nodded, squaring himself against his twin. Poppy couldn't help but think of dueling gunslingers.

"But it's *not* Dylan," said Poppy. "We know now. It's the house. It's always the house." She glanced at Matilda and Irving, who were clinging to each other a few steps farther inside the tent, their faces panicked.

And then they started to change.

Their skin grew waxy. Little plastic ears rose up from their heads. Eye sockets darkened and sank into their skulls. And their mouths pulled back in awful grimaces, this time showing sharp white teeth. Their spines straightened and their limbs stiffened and twitched.

"No, no, no," Poppy whimpered. "It's my fault. I was wrong. Don't do this to them."

Azumi grabbed Poppy and Dash and pulled them away from the two remaining Specials. The three now stood between two dangers: the ghostly orphans in the tent with them, and Dylan, who was laughing with glee from several yards up the new midway outside. And beyond him, from up the hill, Larkspur House, with its darkened windows, seemed to watch with cold confidence, as if it had known all along how this would play out.

"Come on," said Azumi intensely, tugging at her friends' arms. "We need to *run*."

"Where?" asked Poppy. "There's nowhere to go."

"Sure there is," said Dash, pointing up the hill past his brother and the other frozen clowns. "We go forward."

Poppy blinked. "But the house—"

Matilda and Irving raised their arms, reaching for the group. Poppy spun to find Dylan steadying himself.

All at once, Dash and Azumi leapt over the prize counter and then bolted from the tent. Poppy slipped on the grass as she tried to keep up. "Wait!" she cried. But thunder rolled across the meadow again, drowning out her voice. She felt fingertips slide down her spine as Matilda and Irving ran after her, clawing at her tank top, monsters again. She scrambled to her feet and then swung her bag around onto her back.

Ahead, Azumi skirted around Dylan as he jolted toward Dash. "Stay together!" Poppy called out. Dash ducked into his brother's leap, shoving his shoulder into Dylan's gut and throwing him to the ground. It was a vicious move. Poppy cringed.

Azumi headed toward the four clown figurines who were blocking the path farther up the midway. There was no space between them and the tents on either side. The only way through was a gap in the middle where Dylan had stepped forward.

Poppy could hear Matilda and Irving scrambling across the grass behind her. Only a few feet ahead, Dash struggled to stand up as Dylan flailed his arms from the ground nearby, trying to snatch at his brother. Poppy careened toward them, reaching for Dash's shoulder and using her momentum to bring him up.

Dash grunted a thank-you. Then he yelled, "Azumi, watch out!"

Poppy watched the four clowns turn their heads toward Azumi as she crossed through their barricade. In an instant, they were grabbing at Azumi. "No!" she squealed as they pulled her down to the ground.

Poppy wasn't thinking as she slipped the strap of her messenger bag up over her head. "Watch out, Dash," she said, shoving him out of the way. Poppy spun, catching the nylon strap as it slipped down to her hand, the weighted bag like a trebuchet sling as it rocketed around. The bag crunched into the plaster clowns, scattering their broken bodies into the grass around a wide-eyed Azumi.

"Come on, Azumi," said Dash. "Up we go." Barely slowing, he scooped her under her arms to get her running again.

Poppy swung the strap back over her head and across her chest and took off after her friends.

Wind whipped through the corridor of tents as dark clouds swirled and flashed overhead. The spikes on the rooftop seemed to grow and sharpen like syringes. The house was furious with them, Poppy knew. They weren't supposed to win these games. And though they'd just gained some ground with Aloysius and the cough drop, she couldn't let go of how close she'd come to setting *all* the Specials free.

Poppy's lungs clenched painfully as she sprinted from the three ghostly kids. She almost slowed as she saw that the path only led straight back toward the house. But then she heard someone calling out her name from far ahead, beyond the place where Dash and Azumi were sprinting. Was it the wind? Or was the voice only in her head?

Then she saw it. Several yards up the slope, one of the tent flaps on the right side of the midway was open, light emanating from within. "This way!" she called out to Dash and Azumi.

"No way!" said Dash, when he noticed the direction she was leading them. "I'm not going inside again."

As they approached the triangular gleam that spilled out onto the grass, Poppy felt some tension melt from her shoulders. Within the tent, she could see several tall frames set up, glass glistening, reflecting a golden light. An electric sign over the flap flickered to life: *Mirror Maze*.

As they came closer to the open flap, the image of a girl appeared, watching from *inside* one of the tall frames. She looked like a reflection of someone standing by the tent's entry, but Poppy knew better. The girl wore a black dress with a white pinafore over it, wide pockets open by her waist. Her dark hair was tucked back behind her ears. The girl raised a hand and waved repeatedly, a desperate flicker that pulled Poppy forward.

Poppy hoped Dash and Azumi now understood.

The voice she'd heard calling to her from the midway hadn't been the wind playing tricks. It had been her oldest friend, her Girl in the mirror, trying to save her one more time. "Look!" she yelled, her voice ragged from running. "It's Connie! She's found us another way out of here!"

CHAPTER 9

"POPPY, STOP!" DASH cried out. "What if it's another trick—"

But Poppy veered toward the open flap and the flickering red sign.

Azumi chased after them. The Girl in the entry was waving, but Azumi sensed that something was wrong.

Why was Poppy always the one calling the shots?

Azumi glanced over her shoulder. The cat, the bear, and the clown were only several yards behind them. They snarled and leapt toward her.

There was no time to waver. They either went with the Girl in the mirrors, or they kept running up the midway toward the house. Neither seemed like a very good idea.

Poppy hopped through the entry, and Azumi had to follow.

In the cramped space, Dash barreled into Azumi. All three knocked into one of the mirrors, which wobbled precariously.

Outside, Matilda, Irving, and Dylan howled in anger, their voices rising like the wind. They raced forward, quickly closing the space between themselves and the mirror tent. Their heads were tilted back, their plastic mouths open wide now as if hungry. Azumi crouched down and covered her ears with her hands to block out the piercing noise. She didn't want to see what was coming, couldn't imagine what it would feel like when they came through the entry, but she was too frightened to look away.

Hands clamped on her shoulders, yanking her backward as the tent flap dropped down, sealing itself to the ground. Azumi landed on her rear in the cool, soft grass. The canvas rustled for several seconds before stopping abruptly.

Glancing up, Azumi found Poppy panting, staring at the wall as if the canvas might tear open.

Seconds slipped by as Azumi held her breath. This tent was strangely quiet. Finally, when it looked like the Specials couldn't get in, she stood. The tall mirrors on either side of the entry created the illusion of a tunnel stretching into the distance in opposite directions. In the glass were infinite versions of Azumi, Dash, and Poppy staring back at themselves, looking terrified and confused. A string of dim globes hung overhead. Reflected endlessly, they looked like millions of little moons.

But where had Poppy's Girl gone?

"You've gotten us trapped inside *two* of these stupid tents now, Poppy," said Dash, glaring toward the grassy path that bent in an L shape a few yards away.

Poppy glanced around, looking into the mirrors as if for help. "We're out of danger, aren't we?" she said softly. Her voice was stiff with guilt.

"That's the thing," said Dash. "We don't know if we *are* or if we *aren't*. If we'd stayed on our path to the driveway—"

"We *saved* Aloysius," Poppy interrupted. "Isn't that worth something?"

Dash's gaze darkened. "Dylan would have been worth *more*."

Poppy pursed her lips, as if answering him might be as dangerous as meeting one of the Specials in this glimmering corridor.

"Hey!" Azumi snapped her fingers between them. "We're still together. And that's saying a whole lot. Let's just . . . keep moving." Her voice echoed into the distance, as if her many reflections were mocking her.

"Azumi's right," said Poppy. She nodded toward the bend in the maze. "Connie's in here somewhere. She'll lead the way."

As Dash followed Poppy, he glanced at Azumi with a look that told her he was losing patience. But before Azumi could respond, something in the mirror caught her eye.

When she turned to look, the tunnel of reflection had disappeared. In its place was a forest. All around her, daylight filtered through the twisted, moss-covered trees. It was the forest in Japan where she'd last seen her sister.

Azumi was unable to move. From the corner of her eye, she noticed Poppy and Dash continuing on without her. *Again.*

Something pounded at the frame behind her. When she turned, Azumi almost jumped out of her skin. Moriko was there, palms pressed against the glass, her eyes wide and fearful. Azumi covered her eyes and shook her head. "No," she whispered to herself. "Not again." She knew it was the creature, hiding inside her sister's skin, trying to scare her and feed on her fear.

Moriko's voice echoed through the corridor. "Leave the path, Azumi. Run . . ." Even behind her eyelids, the voice made Azumi's skin tingle.

This one sounded . . . frightened. Really, truly *frightened.*

Taking her hands away from her face, Azumi gazed into Moriko's eyes. They were dark brown—not the amber gold that the creature's had been.

There was a stinging behind the bridge of Azumi's nose, tears threatening to fall. *This* was Moriko. Or her spirit, at least. Recognition buzzed Azumi's bones. *"Moriko,"* she whispered, her voice choked. "I'm so sorry. I need you with me now. Please!"

52

"Leave the path, Azumi," Moriko repeated, desperate. "Get out. Run . . ."

Azumi shuddered. "But how?"

The ground began to tremble. Moriko reached out to Azumi. Azumi reached back, her hands smacking the glass. Then something strange happened to Moriko's face. Her eyes seemed to bulge and then droop, pooling near her bottom lid and oozing down her cheeks. Her lips twisted into a sneer before smearing toward her chin and dripping like melting wax, dragging open in a long, silent howl.

Azumi's scream resounded through the mirror maze.

Soon, the rest of Moriko's body appeared to slip and streak down the glass, as the forest all around them liquefied like a sand castle in rough surf. Within seconds, the landscape had transformed back into the dark reflection, the little globes of light dangling overhead, stretching into the endless distance.

"Moriko!" Azumi cried out, slamming her fists against the mirror again and again. But her sister was gone.

CHAPTER 10

AZUMI'S TERRIFIED SHOUTING stopped Dash in his tracks. She was several yards behind him, pounding on one of the mirrors as if she were trying to smash through it and get at something on the other side.

He ran to her and pulled her away from the glass. To his surprise, she clasped his neck and shoved her face into his shoulder, her body heaving with sobs.

Thunder smashed overhead, and a sudden downpour rattled the tent's canvas roof. The rain was so loud, it almost drowned out Azumi's voice as she muttered, "My sister . . . My sister . . ."

"It's okay," Poppy said, coming up behind Dash, making him jump. "We're all together. Now what *about* your sister?"

Azumi's face was already blotchy, but now it turned red. "I saw her in the mirror. She stood in the forest we visited in Japan, where she got lost. She told me to . . . *to leave the path*. To get out. To run . . . And then . . . And then she . . ." Her voice hitched and then rose. "She melted!"

"We already told you," said Dash softly. "It's the house. That wasn't your sister."

Azumi shook her head. "But I think it was. Her eyes were brown. I think her message was a real warning."

"Leave the path?" Poppy repeated. "What does that mean? What path?"

Dash shook his head. "Doesn't matter," he said. "We can't trust *anything* we see here anymore. It's only the house trying to get us back inside so it can drive us insane and slurp up our fear . . ."

"But what if Azumi's right?" Poppy asked. "What if it *was* a message from Moriko's spirit? The *real* Moriko. What if she melted because Larkspur was trying to stop her from communicating with Azumi?"

"And what if that's what Larkspur *wants* you to think?" asked Dash. "Remember what happened in the games tent, Poppy? We need to stick to our *own* plan—get to the driveway and get out!"

"Look around," said Poppy. "We can't get to the driveway right now."

"My point exactly," said Dash, narrowing his eyes.

Poppy sighed. "According to the sign outside, we're in a mirror maze. Mazes have entries and exits. We just have to find the way out."

"You're talking as if reality applies here," Dash argued. "It doesn't."

"C'mon," said Poppy. "What would Marcus have said? I bet he'd have wanted to try and beat the house's game."

"Should we leave a bread-crumb trail?" asked Dash.

Poppy raised her eyebrows. "You have bread crumbs?"

Dash rolled his eyes. "That was a joke."

"It was my sister," said Azumi. "She was talking to *me*. Maybe I should get a say this time."

"But you're . . ." Poppy clamped her mouth shut.

"I'm *what*?" asked Azumi.

Poppy shook her head, as if her thoughts had suddenly flown away. She wasn't sure what she'd almost said. But Poppy knew she needed Azumi's support, especially since Dash was starting to doubt her.

Azumi took Poppy's arm roughly and then pulled her farther into the tunnel of mirrors. Ahead, the path forked. "Which way?" asked Azumi, her voice cold.

Dash followed them slowly, stepping carefully. He wore a smirk, as if he was amused that Poppy might be losing her leader position.

A word slipped into Poppy's mind: *mutiny.*

Something flickered in Poppy's vision—a dark fluttering in one of the mirrors to the right. Her heart leapt and she rushed forward. "Connie!" she cried out, dragging Azumi along with her.

Dash ran to keep up. "Poppy, slow down!" he yelled.

"She's helping us! She'll lead the way." The shadow began to fade. "Connie! Connie, wait!"

The trio ventured into the new passage. Ahead, the mirrors formed a wide, circular clearing. Several openings led off toward tunnels like legs from a spider's body. At the center of the new space, the mirror frames turned their reflections kaleidoscopic. Hundreds of themselves stared back, all focused in different directions, making the doorways hidden, almost invisible.

"Connie," Poppy whispered. "Which way?"

"I hate to be the one to point this out," said Dash, "but what if your *cousin* is leading us the wrong way?"

"She wouldn't do that," said Poppy.

Azumi spoke up quietly. "I thought the same thing about Moriko."

Poppy ignored them. "Connie, please!" A single shadow appeared near a doorway on the far side of the space. Poppy pointed. "There . . . see?"

Consolida's pale face was visible briefly before it began to twitch and thrash, just as her reflections had done since

Poppy had arrived at Larkspur. Of course, the house didn't want Connie helping. "Look!" Poppy said. "The exit!"

"You're not listening to anything we're saying," said Dash, keeping up as Poppy moved across the space.

"The house *wants* us to argue. We need to be on the same page."

"*Your* page, you mean," said Dash, his voice rising.

Well, yeah! thought Poppy. *My ancestors lived here. Connie and Cyrus were* my *cousins. If any of us should be in charge, it should be the one with the connection to Larkspur House. Me!*

Poppy felt her body jolt, realizing what she'd just thought. This wasn't like her. Maybe the others were right, and she needed to step back and listen to them for a change.

Not if you wish to leave, said a voice in her head, a voice that sounded like her own.

"Hold on," said Azumi. "If Connie is over there, then who's that?" She nodded toward a different exit. Poppy turned to find another figure standing there, also waving. She was wearing the same black dress with the white pinafore, and she twitched in a rhythm similar to the first girl.

Poppy's face burned. "I . . . I don't know."

"And there," said Dash, pointing toward yet another of the doorways. A third Connie watched them, twitching and waving, as if trying to get them to approach her too.

"What in the . . . ?" Poppy's heart began to pound. She glanced back at the first Connie, who flickered and flinched, raising both hands over her head, desperate now.

"Oh, no," said Azumi, turning slowly, observing what was happening in the mirrors. Now every frame contained an image of Poppy's Girl in the mirrors. Each of them raised two hands, mimicking the first Connie, then started to move, and twitched and blurred. The reflections flooded the room with endless Connies. There were too many of them to tell them apart.

"We need to leave," Dash whispered. "Now."

"But which way do we go?" asked Azumi.

"The house is trying to confuse us," said Poppy. "We just need to figure out which Connie is the real one."

"How?" asked Dash, crossing his arms, trying to control his trembling.

"Their eyes," said Poppy. "The fake ones will have golden irises. We just need a closer look." She rushed toward the side of the circular space where she'd first noticed her Girl appear. But as she got closer, she realized that the blurred figures were shaking too hard for her to see details in their faces. "Connie, please, let me know which one is you," Poppy pleaded.

Except for the sound of the rain hitting the roof, the room was eerily quiet.

Cautiously, Poppy approached the one standing beside an

exit that she thought might've been the first. To Poppy's surprise, the girl in the mirror suddenly froze, her face darkened by shadow. "Please," Poppy whispered, reaching out toward the reflection, which stood beside her own. "Show me your eyes."

But the figure did not open her eyes. Instead, a dark line creased across the bottom half of her face, curving into a wide, demented smile. Thin lips parted, revealing a mouth crowded with teeth that were jagged pieces of broken glass.

Poppy screamed and stumbled back. Behind her, Dash and Azumi let out terrified shrieks that resounded off the mirrors. Looking around, Poppy noticed that all the Connies were grinning in the same horrible way. They opened their mouths, their teeth sparkling, and then they all stepped forward onto the grass, their bodies pulling away from the frames like black mercury. They solidified into an army of shadows, reached toward Poppy, Azumi, and Dash, and then, all at once, they rushed forward.

CHAPTER 11

DASH GRABBED AZUMI'S arm and then raced toward Poppy as the mass of mirror girls began to close in on them. He shoved the others through the nearest opening as whispers of fingertips brushed against his back. Poppy stumbled slightly, and he shouted out, "Go! Go! Go!" She reached out to the mirrors on either side to steady herself. Then, without looking back, she bolted forward.

The string of dim lights led the way down the corridor and the walls seemed to constrict. Ahead, there was another fork.

Dash groaned. There was no time to consider which direction would be best. What if they chose a path that took them to a dead end? There were shards of glass teeth inside the girls' mouths! Dash tried to put the image out of his mind, but it was stuck. The girls would swarm, and then . . .

Poppy flew down the left path at the fork. Dash and Azumi followed.

Dash could hear Dylan's voice in his head, telling him to buck up, straighten out, get strong. *You've come this far. You'll find the way to get out.*

They ran and ran. And suddenly, it hit him. *Get out.* That's what Moriko's reflection had said to Azumi only minutes earlier. She'd said something else . . .

A whooshing sound echoed through the corridor as the crowd of girls came faster and faster. *What else had she said . . . ?* Dash felt his lungs ache as he struggled for breath.

Get off the path . . .

They were on a path right now. *This* was the path that Moriko had meant.

But how were they supposed to get off it without exiting the maze first?

Thunder crashed, and the mirror frames rattled.

Get off the path . . .

A lesson from an old tutor flashed into Dash's memory. Something from a poem.

The best way out is . . . *through!*

"Poppy!" he shouted. "Your bag!"

Ahead, Poppy glanced over her shoulder, the messenger bag still bouncing at her hip. "What about it?" she called back.

"Use it to smash the mirrors!"

She kept running. "How?"

The grass rustled behind them, trampled by hundreds of shadowy feet.

"Swing it like you did at the clowns!"

A T-shaped fork appeared in the path, a complete stop that branched to their left and right. In the mirrors, Dash could see his group racing toward this wall, fear painted across their faces. Just behind them was a flickering wave of darkness, threatening to crash over them. Thousands of specks glimmered like stars—the girls' glass-shard teeth caught the light from above as their grins widened further.

"Do it, now!" Dash yelled.

Poppy lifted the strap over her head and spun as she sprinted, the weight from the bag carrying her forward even faster. It hit the mirror with a hard *crack*, and the glass in one of the frames splintered. A muffled shriek echoed down the corridor toward them, as if the mass of girls had somehow felt the hit.

"Again!" Azumi cried out, pausing by Poppy and glancing back. Her eyes widened as she saw the dark wave cresting over their heads. "Hurry, Poppy!"

Dash faced the girls. They poured toward him—a smoky liquid made of shivering hands and teeth and hair. He held out his arms, as if that might be enough to stop them before they could reach Poppy and Azumi.

From the edge of his vision, he watched Azumi help Poppy lift the messenger bag over her head. Quickly, the girls brought the bag back down onto the glass. Their force splintered it further. The wave of Connies shuddered, feeling the blow again. The dark mass slowed, but only for a moment.

"Dash!" Poppy called out. "Help us!" She and Azumi backed up several paces, and Dash moved forward with them.

The three bolted toward the cracked mirror, covering their faces with their hands as they tilted their shoulders toward the glass. Dash heard a fracturing as the glass gave way, and they passed through the jagged wooden frame. He felt himself drop into a wet darkness beyond.

Dash rolled across the sopping grass outside the tent, crunching large glass shards that fell around him. A terrible cry rose up from the mirror maze. As he looked back, he saw cracks race from mirror to mirror. The ghostly girls were all frozen in place, staring with their golden eyes out at Azumi, Poppy, and him.

Then the frames exploded inward, the glass ripping into the shadowy mass of girls. All at once, the phantoms disappeared, their sharp teeth mixing with the blast.

The strings of lights flickered out, leaving Dash, Poppy, and Azumi lying in the meadow's pitch-darkness.

CHAPTER 12

DRIZZLE CAME DOWN from the thick clouds overhead. Lightning flashed, giving Azumi a brief glimpse of the tent from which she'd tumbled. To her surprise, its wall was solid again, the dark stripes looking like tall figures staring down at her. She scrambled backward, scraping her palms on tiny bits of broken glass scattered on the ground.

Poppy and Dash were already rising to their feet. They held out their hands to help her up. No one said a word as they turned and ran from the fairgrounds.

Leave the path, Azumi . . . Get out. Run.

Moriko! Her sister had been in there. She had tried to help. And it hadn't been a trick!

Maybe that's what the house wants you to think . . .

Shut up, shut up!

Another flash, and the house appeared on the hill to their left. One corner of it was closer now, but they still had a ways to go before they reached the driveway, especially if they kept on their path along the edge of the woods.

The wind whipped at them, and Azumi's long dress caught the gust like a sail, almost knocking her backward. Dash and Poppy fought to push forward.

At least they were heading in the right direction.

How much more of this can you take before you shatter into bits . . . just like the mirrors?

Azumi stopped running. *Get out of my head!*

Laughter swirled around her. Shaking with fear, she glanced about, seeking its source. But the sound almost seemed to be part of the storm itself. The tents were already far behind them. And ahead . . . Poppy and Dash were still running through the tall grass.

"Hey!" Azumi shouted out. "Wait for me!"

As they paused to look back, a blinding shock of electricity struck the ground just yards in front of where they were standing. Poppy and Dash flew into the air and landed on their backs. Azumi gasped and rushed toward them.

They both stared up at the sky, rain rinsing across their faces.

No! Please! Don't be dead! Don't be DEAD!

She yelped when they blinked. "Oh my goodness," she said. "Are you okay?"

Poppy blinked. "I think I am." She patted herself down as if searching for an injury. "Dash?"

Dash tried to stand up. "That was close."

Rising, Poppy hugged Azumi. "You saved us. If we'd kept going in that direction . . . I don't want to know what we'd look like right now."

"We have to get out of this storm," said Azumi.

Another bolt of lightning split the sky overhead, followed immediately by a deafening crack of thunder.

"Get out of the storm?" Dash echoed. "How? Go back into Larkspur?"

"Look!" Poppy pointed toward the woods. Near the trees, there was a dark structure that looked like it might be a small barn or stable. "Maybe in there."

Dash shook his head violently. "I'm not following you into another building."

A flash of lightning and roll of thunder shook the earth. When the wind gusted, some of the tree branches brushed the ground.

"We don't have a choice," said Poppy, grabbing Azumi's hand. "If we stay out here, we'll die."

"The house doesn't want to kill us," Dash insisted. "It only wants to scare us. Our fear is giving it fuel. If we *die*, it loses too."

"Tell that to Marcus!" Poppy shouted, shocking everyone into a momentary silence.

Dash clutched at his skull. "Poppy . . ."

But Poppy had already started away from him, pulling Azumi roughly behind her. Azumi yanked herself back. Poppy shook her head and then stomped onward, leaving them behind. Azumi held her hand out to Dash instead. "We need to stay together. You said it yourself. Remember?"

CHAPTER 13

AS HE HIKED across the meadow, Dash could still feel electricity tingling through his body. Was this what Dylan had experienced when—

Dash squeezed the thought away.

He hated to admit it, but Poppy was right. The idea of staying out in this storm frightened him almost as much as the weird-looking barn.

The building seemed to grow as they struggled through the fierce wind. With each flash of lightning, Dash could see more details. Ragged holes gaped in the rotting roof. The wooden walls that held it up were ancient and tilted. One good gust might knock the whole thing down.

Poppy was not slowing her pace. Dash was growing frustrated arguing with her. Something had happened to her when the creature had killed Marcus. In Poppy's mind, *her* ideas were the only ones worth anything. The shy girl he'd met early that morning was gone.

A wide doorway stood open in the buckling wall of the barn, and Poppy and Azumi huddled just inside. There didn't appear to be a door attached anymore, which was a relief. Nothing could swing shut and trap them inside.

None of us is the same as we were this morning. He heard Dylan's voice in his ear. Especially *not you, little brother.*

"When did you get so wise?" Dash whispered, as if his brother could hear him.

"Who are you talking to?" Azumi asked him as he took cover from the wind and rain and stood beside them.

"Me, myself, and I," Dash murmured, glancing into the darkened space. He turned on his phone's flashlight, revealing damp spots on the dirt floor where water puddled, dripping from the ceiling. Rain drummed on the roof, and the wind creaked the structure's old bones. Open stalls lined the left wall. Straw was piled against the partitions like snowdrifts. The musky smell of damp livestock stung his sinuses.

A squeal echoed around the space, and Dash jumped backward through the doorway. Swinging his light to the left, he saw Poppy climbing a rickety set of stairs. His face burned. "You've got to be kidding," he called out to her.

"I thought I heard something," she answered, continuing on.

"*Something?*"

"A voice. Listen."

Dash heard nothing but the rain hitting the roof and his heartbeat pounding in his head. He tried to squash his anger. Yelling at her wouldn't make her hear him any better. "Seems like a good reason to stay down here, don't you think?"

Azumi stood at the bottom of the steps. She glanced over at Dash, looking like she was thinking the same thing. "Can't you do something?" he whispered.

"It sounds like a recording," Poppy called out. "Or the radio."

"Be careful, Poppy!" said Azumi. "Should we follow her?"

Dash grimaced, his shoulders aching.

From the loft, Poppy called out, "Oh my gosh, there's a ton of stuff up here."

"There's *a ton of stuff* down here too," said Dash. "None of it means we need to go poking around."

Poppy peered over the ledge at him, her mouth pressed into a scowl. "But we still need to figure out how to free the rest of the Specials."

Dash couldn't help flinching. "The Specials? I thought we were hiding from the storm. We're heading back to the driveway. Remember?"

She went on, her voice hardening. "There might be something up here that'll help release Matilda and Irving."

"And my brother? We still care about him, right?"

"If we run into them again, we need to be prepared," Poppy answered. Maybe she hadn't heard him? She nodded at the doorway, where the rain was coming down in sheets. "And we're kind of stuck in here for now."

Azumi began to climb the steps.

A sudden sense of loneliness closed in around Dash. If Dylan were here, they would stand up for each other. Before he knew what he was doing, he too was on the stairs.

Once he'd reached the top, he could hear the voice that Poppy had mentioned. It had a droning quality, but it was too soft for him to make out any words.

The roof was pitched sharply against the left edge of the platform. In the center of the flooring, a red wool blanket had been laid out, as if someone's picnic had been interrupted and they'd left before they'd planned to. A few dust-encrusted bags were lying around the blanket in a misshapen circle. This was where the sound was coming from.

Dash shone his phone's flashlight on a small wooden rectangle in the middle of the blanket. On its lower half someone had written the alphabet, and the words *YES* and *NO*. In its center were the words *Shadow Board*.

"People use them to talk to ghosts," said Azumi.

"I know what a Ouija board is," said Dash.

Poppy knelt on the blanket.

But Azumi shouted, "Don't touch it!" Poppy flinched.

Poppy shook her head. "Okay. We've been talking to ghosts just fine by ourselves."

She grabbed one of the dusty bags and unzipped it. Reaching inside, she removed what looked like a tape deck. From a small speaker, the droning, warped voice grew much louder, bouncing around the loft. "A cassette recorder," said Poppy, pressing the stop button. "Almost dead." Digging in the same bag, she produced a couple of notebooks, pens, some Polaroid pictures, and finally, a set of batteries. She slotted the batteries into a panel on the back of the recorder, then hit rewind. "Maybe if we listen from the beginning—"

"We won't be in here that long," Dash interrupted.

"You don't know that," said Poppy. The cassette clicked to an automatic stop as it finished rewinding. She tapped another button, and the recording began to play.

CHAPTER 14

A GIRL'S CHIPPER voice rattled the tape recorder's speaker. *"Note to self,"* she said. *"Find a new group of friends, preferably ones that aren't immature weirdos."*

"It's a little loud," said Dash.

Poppy fiddled with the volume knob and accidentally hit the fast-forward button. When she pressed play again, another voice spoke—a different girl with a velvety and frightened warble: *"But I read somewhere that the orphanage director's father was the one who built the house. He was a famous artist. I think his name was Frederick Caldwell. Some of his work used to hang in the library in Greencliffe. Lots of landscapes. But he also did portraits. I've heard that there was something weird about his work."*

Nervous laughter erupted from the speaker, and then a boy spoke up. *"What kind of weird?"*

"*Not sure. But you're supposed get a spooky feeling from looking at the paintings.*"

"*I get a spooky feeling from looking at your mother!*" said the boy on the tape.

"*Shut up, Will!*" yelled the two girls. Everyone on the tape chuckled.

"*Seriously though,*" said another boy. "*I've heard that too. And the reason is: Frederick Caldwell made a pact with something that lives in these woods.*"

"*A pact?*" asked the first girl.

"*Uh-huh. My grandfather said there was a secret society down in New York City who told Frederick what to do. Where to build the house. How to contact the . . . thing that could help make him richer and more famous. But there was a cost. That's why the painter's family died. That's why Frederick ended up going insane. And his son too. This land is cursed. Lots of people died here.*"

There was a brief pause, and then the first girl said, "*I'm so glad we came!*" Sarcasm dripped from her voice.

Azumi pressed the stop button, and Dash and Poppy jumped.

Wide-eyed, Poppy spoke up. "I knew we came up here for a reason! These kids' stories! A pact? It's like someone wanted us to—" Azumi touched the rewind button for a second, and Poppy flinched. "What are you doing?"

"Listen," whispered Azumi, turning on the recording again.

The voices started up. "—*son too. This land is cursed. Lots of people died here.*" There was the pause, followed by: "*I'm so glad we came!*"

"What are we listening for?" asked Dash.

Azumi shook her head, rewound the tape a little, and hit play one more time.

"—*is cursed. Lots of people died here.*" She flicked the volume back up, and suddenly Poppy heard something else inside that small pause. Another voice. A deeper voice. It said: "*You'll . . . die . . . too . . .*"

And then that chipper voice went on, "*I'm so glad we came!*"

Azumi pressed stop and looked at Poppy and Dash. "You heard it?" Stone-faced, Poppy and Dash nodded. "Who *were* these kids?" Azumi asked.

Dash glanced down at the blanket, picking up the notebooks and photographs that Poppy had taken from one of the bags. A Polaroid fell to the floor—a picture of four kids, smiling as they stood before what looked like the gate of Larkspur House. The group in the photo were dressed in clothes that might have been stylish forty years earlier. The two girls had long hair and the boys wore shiny shirts with giant collars.

"They probably came up from Greencliffe to explore Larkspur," said Poppy.

"I don't think they ever left," said Azumi, her brow creased.

"Five of them," Poppy said, nodding at the backpacks and bags lying around the shadow board.

"But there are only four in the photo," said Dash.

"One of them had to take the picture," Poppy went on. "*Five*. The same number as Cyrus's first orphans in the 1930s who drowned. The same number of the Specials in the 1950s."

"And *us*," said Azumi. "There were five of us too. Before Marcus and Dylan—"

"It's the house," said Dash quickly. "It's like . . . it keeps calling five kids. Over and over. Like five is its lucky number."

"A *powerful* number," said Azumi. "My baaba used to talk about how certain numbers have special meanings."

"So what's it mean right now?" asked Dash. Azumi shook her head. The diamond-shaped piece of wood rattled in the center of the shadow board, catching everyone's attention. His eyes popped wide. "Was that you guys?"

The girls whispered, "No."

All three of them scooted away from the board.

To their surprise, the wooden pointer began to slowly slide around, pausing on certain letters. Azumi read them aloud. "L . . . O . . . O . . . K . . ." The pointer stopped moving.

"They're here," said Poppy, her eyes flicking around the darkness of the loft.

"*Look?*" Dash said, staring at the shadow board.

"They want to talk to us," said Poppy. "Just like the first orphans did, in the classroom with the chalkboard."

"Yeah, but didn't those kids try to drown you and Marcus?" asked Azumi.

Dash poked at the pointer. "What do they want us to look at?" He glanced around as if trying to find this new group of spirits. "Hello? Could you be a little more clear?"

"Oh my goodness," said Poppy, glancing down at the notebooks she'd taken from one of the bags, sliding out a thin piece of paper onto the blanket. "Check this out." It was a yellowed newspaper clipping dated 1912. She read: *"Greencliffe, Jun. 1. An early-morning fire in the upper floors of Larkspur House resulted in the deaths of two members of the Caldwell family today . . ."* Poppy looked up at the others. "It's the same story we found back in the tower of the house. That page was torn off halfway through, but this one . . ." She unfolded the bottom part of the paper, revealing the rest of the article. "This one is whole."

The wooden pointer slid across the word *YES* several times before skidding to a stop.

"What's the article say, Poppy?" Azumi asked.

Dash shone his flashlight onto the page so Poppy could see better.

Poppy read more. *"The boy is currently under observation at the new Peekskill Hospital south of Greencliffe."* She looked up. "The

79

boy was Cyrus, remember? The painter was his father." She went on, "*This is the second tragic event to strike Larkspur House recently. Only one month ago, several visitors were killed when their car crashed into the wall inside the main gate at Hardscrabble Road. Those victims were Mrs. Dagmar Spencer, age 40, of New York City, and her five young wards: Fergus Spencer, age 11; Gustav Spencer, age 9; Kristof Spencer, age 10; Dawn Spencer, age 12; and Tatum Spencer, age 11. Their driver, Blake Brazzel, was thrown from the car and sustained only minor injuries. He claimed that he lost control of the wheel. Mrs. Spencer, a self-proclaimed psychic medium, had reportedly been invited to the house with her children by Mrs. Eugenia Caldwell for a Spiritualist ceremony. The investigation into that accident is ongoing.*"

"Five more dead kids," said Azumi. "This house is hungry."

"What's a *Spiritualist ceremony*?" asked Dash.

"Something to do with psychics," said Poppy. "Maybe this Mrs. Spencer and her children held a séance for Mrs. Caldwell?"

"Why did *these* kids want us to know about this?" asked Azumi.

Dash folded his arms. "What if it's all a distraction? What if they're working with the house to confuse us?"

"By giving us *more* information?" said Poppy, sounding confident. "I don't think so. They want to help."

"But what if their help is the kind that hurts?"

Azumi nodded at the stairs. "We're only here until the storm breaks . . . until it's safe for us to leave again and find the driveway."

Poppy began to rummage through the other bags. When she opened the heaviest one, she discovered a large tool—two metal handles that swung apart and a sharp pair of blades that opened and closed like a bird's beak. "A bolt cutter," said Poppy.

"Maybe they meant for us to find this," Dash said, taking the cutter from her.

The pointer slid across the board again. Azumi called the letters. "L . . . I . . . S . . . T . . . E . . . N . . ."

The cassette player on the blanket by Poppy's knees whirred to life again as the tape sped forward all by itself, and Poppy jumped away from it. The cassette stopped and then began to play at a normal speed. Screaming erupted from the speaker, the kids' voices overlapping in a frenzied panic. Then, drowning out everything else, a familiar sound roared—a snarling howl.

It was the creature!

Poppy clapped her hands to her ears, but what came next was too loud to block out—a sudden crunching sound followed by a horrible silence. The player stopped abruptly, the buttons of the machine snapping up as the deck popped open, tossing the tape onto the blanket between them.

CHAPTER 15

CHILLS COATED AZUMI'S skin, like the water that was still dripping from the roof of the barn overhead.

She stared down at the cassette. It made her wonder what she might have left in the house that someone would find someday—evidence that she'd been here.

She closed her eyes, only to see Marcus flying through the air, right before he hit the tree, and the creature watching the rest of them run away. Icy guilt ran through her veins as the image looped through her brain like a glitch, before it melted into a vision of her sister lying motionless on the mossy ground in the Japanese forest.

She pressed her palms into her eye sockets. The burst of purple and green that appeared in the blackness behind her eyelids kept her from thinking about what must have happened to the five kids from Greencliffe after they'd encountered the shadow creature that lurked in these woods.

The pointer continued to slowly slide around the shadow board, hovering over the same letters, again and again. L . . . I . . . S . . . T . . . E . . . N . . . L . . . I . . . S . . . T . . . E . . . N . . . L . . . I . . . S . . . T . . . E . . . N . . .

"What are we supposed to hear?" asked Poppy.

"The rain," whispered Azumi. "It's stopped."

Dash swung the bolt cutter and pointed it at the shadow board. "They're telling us to leave."

Poppy started, "I don't think that's what they're—"

"I don't care what you think," said Dash, standing. "Azumi's right. There's no more rain. It's time to go."

"You don't need to talk to me like that, Dash," said Poppy. "I'm only trying to figure out—"

"Stop!" said Azumi. She shook her head, clutching her arms across her rib cage. "Stop fighting!" Dash and Poppy stared at her, their cheeks burning. "I really want to go home. We need to find the way out."

"We all want that, Azumi," said Dash, suddenly concerned. "We're going to get there."

"Some of us don't have a home," whispered Poppy. "Some of us thought *this* place would become home."

"If you want to stay so bad, I'm sure your ancestors would

be happy to have you," said Dash. "You could keep Dylan company."

Poppy glared at him. She gathered up the tape and the recorder, then stomped toward the stairs.

"Am I wrong?" Dash took Azumi's hand and pulled her to her feet. "We already decided that Dylan's too lost to save. He has to stay here. *We* don't, thank goodness. But you keep finding ways to stop us, Poppy. First, the games tent. Then the mirror maze. Now we're in a barn, talking to ghosts again, instead of looking for the driveway."

At the bottom of the staircase, Poppy crossed her arms and looked up at them. "That's not fair." Her voice was surprisingly calm. It was almost creepy. Was something controlling her? Azumi wondered. "I'm not the only one making choices here," Poppy went on. Dash scoffed, throwing back his head. "*You* decided to move on without Dylan. Not me, Dash. I haven't told you to do anything."

Azumi edged her way carefully down the steps. Dash was close behind. It felt like she was caught in the middle of an argument between her parents. She *wished* her parents were here. Then she wouldn't have to be the mediator between these two. The bickering was becoming exhausting.

"Come on," said Dash, brushing by Poppy and heading toward the wide doorway out toward the meadow.

Lightning flashed, framing the doorway outside as a blinding rectangle that burned Azumi's eyes.

Three figures stood in the distance, a dozen yards up the grassy hill. Watching. Three masks—the bear, the cat, and the clown—there and then gone.

"What's wrong?" Poppy asked.

"They're out there," said Azumi. "Dylan and the Specials. I saw them."

"I don't see anything," said Dash, raising the sharp end of the bolt cutter toward the night. "Do you, Poppy?"

Poppy shook her head, then glanced at Azumi as if she should be worried.

Great, Azumi thought. Now *they start to agree.*

CHAPTER 16

STAY NEAR THE *trees*, Azumi thought. *Stay hidden. They can see you. They can see everything that happens here.*

Every few steps, whenever Poppy and Dash weren't looking, she glanced over her shoulder. She sensed that Matilda, Irving, and Dylan were close behind her, but she couldn't make them out. And she didn't want Poppy and Dash to think she was seeing things again.

The driveway had to be coming up soon. Unless the land was stretching out before them, getting longer, like the hallways inside . . . Maybe Larkspur would never allow them to reach it.

Her sister's voice echoed in her mind. *Leave the path . . .*

"There *is* no path," Azumi whispered.

"Did you say something?" asked Dash. Azumi shook her head, staring at the ground.

"What's that?" Poppy froze and pointed ahead. A light was glowing several yards into the woods.

"A flashlight?" Dash suggested. "Is someone there?"

"Shh," said Poppy. "They might hear us."

"It's not a flashlight," said Azumi. "It's flickering. Like a flame. Look. The shadows of the trees are moving. "

"Let's get away from here," said Dash, stepping out into the meadow.

The sounds of the storm continued to blow across the landscape, and Azumi listened hard for the footsteps she knew were coming behind them. Wind rattled branches. Water dropped from the leaves, spattering the ground below. But underneath all of that, there was another sound.

It was music. And it was coming from the place in the woods where the light was shining.

"Is that what I think it is?" asked Dash. "Marcus?"

"It's his uncle's melody," said Poppy. She glanced at the others, as if seeking their permission. "Should we check it out?" A moment later, she and Dash headed toward the light.

Azumi scrambled to follow.

As they moved through the trees, they saw that the glow was coming from an antique lamp hanging on the wall of a large shed. Orange flame danced inside the glass. A door stood open beside it, and the tune echoed out from the darkness within.

Dash put away his phone and grabbed the lantern, holding it up to reveal the shed's interior. The rusty walls were made of corrugated tin. A large object sat near the rear wall, covered with a thick cloth.

Before they knew it, all three of them had stepped inside.

Poppy approached the canvas-covered object slowly, and the music grew louder with every step. Dash raised the lantern higher as he followed. She was relieved that he hadn't yet called out for her to stop, that this was a terrible idea, that it must be another trap.

When Poppy reached the object, the canvas buzzed with the melody. She grabbed the edge of the fabric and lifted it slightly. She saw what looked like a flat tire.

The thing under the cloth was a car. The plinking sounds echoed inside its cabin.

"Azumi, will you give me a hand?"

Together, the girls lifted the canvas away, revealing a black, rusted hull. A whiff of ancient ash swirled around them. The vehicle looked like an antique, maybe a hundred years old, but its front had been crushed almost flat, and all the windows were gone. The inside of the car had been burned out. Twisted springs poked up from several rows of blackened seats.

"Something's in the back of the car," said Dash, shining the light through a gap where the rear windshield had once been.

Poppy flinched. How had she not noticed the shape sitting there, hidden beneath a white sheet? "Hello?" she said, her voice smaller than she'd meant it to be.

Something was reaching out to her. Something that wanted to help.

A metallic taste tingled at the back of her tongue.

Poppy clutched the doorknob and then swung it open.

"What are you doing?" Azumi cried out.

"That's it," said Dash, moving the lantern away. "I'm out."

"Hold on," said Poppy. Couldn't they understand she had a deeper connection with this place than they did? "Why won't you trust me?"

"Because you keep doing stuff like this!" Dash yelled.

"I trust *you*, Poppy," Azumi said more softly, as if her words were aimed at Dash. "I just don't trust anything else in this place."

Leaning into the cabin, Poppy's eyes began to water. A terrible stench assaulted her sinuses.

The tune went on and on. Up close, Poppy suddenly realized what kind of instrument was making the noise. A music box underneath that white sheet was playing.

"*Listen*," said Poppy, glancing out the windows at Azumi and Dash, who'd paired up near the back of the vehicle. "That's what the recorder was saying. This is what it wanted us to hear."

Dash pursed his lips. Gripping his bolt cutter like a crutch, he placed the lantern on the ground.

Azumi stared in wonder into the car. The music seemed to swell.

Without waiting for an answer, Poppy grabbed the sheet and pulled it away.

CHAPTER 17

DASH BLINKED. THE shed had disappeared. He found himself standing beside a circular table in a sitting room off the large foyer of Larkspur House. The curtains were drawn, and around the room, candelabras flickered orange. Though the space was dim, he could see Poppy and Azumi standing on opposite sides of the table, the three of them forming a triangle. The girls looked as surprised as he felt, their mouths dropped in Os of horror.

They were back inside again!

"What's going on?" he called out to the girls, but they both seemed too shocked to answer.

It was then that Dash noticed they weren't alone. At the head of the table was a woman dressed all in black, a floral cap pinned to her head and a long, thin veil covering her face. Five children were seated around the table, their hands linked, and all five had blindfolds tied around their eyes.

"*What's going on?*" echoed one of the boys.

The woman in the veil shuddered. "Are you hearing the spirits, Gustav?" she asked him. The boy nodded. She glanced at the woman standing beside her and whispered, "We have visitors, Mrs. Caldwell." Mrs. Caldwell clutched at her collar in surprise, her pale face flooding with color. The woman in the veil reached toward the center of the table, where Dash noticed a small, elaborately carved wooden box. She flipped it open and a familiar tune began to play—Marcus's melody plinking out quietly into the space. "A gift from my grandmother," the woman explained. "Music to protect against negative energies that may try to break the children's concentration. It prevents *lies*."

It's a vision, thought Dash. *Like the one Poppy and Marcus experienced in the classroom earlier.*

"Can they see us?" whispered Azumi.

Before Dash or Poppy could respond, one of the blindfolded girls whispered, "*Can they see us?*"

The veiled woman jerked her head around. "We cannot see you. No."

"Who are you?" asked Poppy.

"*Who are you?*" repeated another of the blindfolded girls.

The veiled woman leaned back in her chair. "My name is

Dagmar Spencer. These children are my wards: Fergus, Gustav, Kristof, Dawn, and Tatum. They are special. They translate communications from the beyond. We've come to help Mrs. Caldwell here at Larkspur House."

Here were the psychic medium and the kids who died in the car accident at Larkspur's gate. Dagmar's ruined vehicle had been draped with that dusty canvas in the shack.

Dash tried to slow his breathing as he realized what was going to happen to these people later this day.

"Tell me now," said the veiled woman. "Are you the spirits who have been taunting Mrs. Caldwell's family these past few years?"

"Spirits?" asked Azumi. "Us?"

One of the wards started to repeat her, but Dash spoke up quickly, interrupting. "We haven't been taunting anyone."

"We haven't been taunting anyone," said another of the blindfolded children.

"Oh, no?" Mrs. Caldwell answered, her voice quavering. "Would you please be kind enough to explain the noises we hear every night? Would you tell us why my husband's paintings switch walls and rooms?" She paused, as if trying to hold back tears. "Why do my children wake up screaming?"

"That's not us," said Poppy.

"*That's not us.*"

Dagmar raised her brow and said, "They cannot lie."

Mrs. Caldwell gasped and then held her hand to her mouth. "Then . . . who? *Who* is tormenting my family?"

"Not who," said Azumi, trying to find the words to explain. "More of a . . . *what.*" One of the children echoed her, and Poppy shot her a stern look.

The women glanced nervously at each other. The music box slowed, and Dagmar wound it up again, returning it quickly to the center of the table.

But why did the kids in the loft send us here? Dash wondered. *To find out more about Frederick Caldwell's pact? Maybe even how to break it?*

From somewhere down a darkened hallway, a baby started crying. Poppy flicked her head toward the noise. And that's when Dash caught a glimpse of another little girl standing in the doorway watching the séance.

"Consolida!" Mrs. Caldwell cried out. "What are you doing out of your room? Where is Miss Ada?"

The girl slipped around the corner. Mrs. Caldwell watched anxiously. Pattering footsteps echoed into the distance.

"Connie!" Poppy called out, darting away from the group.

"*Connie!*" one of the children echoed.

Dash reached out for Poppy as she ran past him toward the doorway. "Poppy, wait!" he cried out, before planting his hand over his mouth. He knew what was coming next.

"Poppy, wait!"

"Poppy?" asked Dagmar. "Is that your name?"

But Poppy was already gone, chasing her cousin into the depths of this strange vision.

The music in the box shivered onward.

CHAPTER 18

POPPY RAN, LISTENING to footfalls echoing off the walls of the narrow corridors. She recognized some parts of the house, certain turns of the halls, the position of the stained-glass windows and the sunlight streaming through. The pattering stopped abruptly. "Connie!" she called out again. "Stop!"

Coming around a corner, Poppy yelped. The girl was waiting several feet away, her arms crossed, hugging a cloth doll to her chest. Her brow was set in what looked like a mask of bravery, but Poppy could see the fear in her glistening eyes. A tall mirror in an ornate gold frame hung on the wall just beside them, their reflections only inches away. How bizarre to finally be on the same side of the glass.

Before Poppy could speak, Connie opened her mouth. "Are

you one of Mother's guests? You were supposed to stay with the others."

"And *you* were supposed to stay in your room," Poppy answered with a smirk. Then she realized, the girl was actually speaking with her. A wave of emotion nearly knocked Poppy off her feet. This girl was Poppy's family. Her actual family! Poppy wanted to throw her arms around the girl and squeeze her. But she didn't know what might happen if they touched. Would the vision end? Would Connie disappear again, this time for good? "You can see me?"

"Of course I can see you," said Connie. "Why wouldn't I be able to see you?" Poppy watched the girl's fingers twitching, revealing that she knew *exactly* what Poppy had meant. Connie knew that she wasn't one of her mother's guests. She squinted at Poppy, slipping her doll into one of her wide pockets. "Why were you chasing me?"

"I just wanted to talk to you." Upstairs, the baby's wailing continued. "Is that Cyrus?"

"My little brother." Connie nodded. After a moment, she scrunched up her face. "Who *are* you?" she asked, the words coming slowly, as if she didn't want to know the answer.

Poppy adjusted the strap of her messenger bag and smoothed her purple T-shirt. "My name is Poppy Caldwell. I'm your . . . your cousin."

98

"No, you're not," said Connie sharply. "My cousins live in Colorado and their names are Atticus and Julius."

Poppy's eyes went wide. Atticus and Julius. One of those two boys must have been her own great-grandfather. One of them was her connection to this awful place.

"I'm a . . . *new* cousin," said Poppy. "We've never met before. But trust me. One day, we'll be best friends."

Connie's face dropped. "But Father . . . he doesn't allow me to have friends. He doesn't like us to go far from the house. He says the world is dangerous."

"That's horrible," said Poppy, flinching.

The article about the fire blinked into her mind. According to the newspaper, the psychic medium's car accident had occurred about a month before the nursery fire—*today*. Poppy's skin tingled. Should she tell the girl what she knew? "You can't listen to what he says," she blurted out.

Connie cringed. "But he's my father. I *must* listen to him. Everyone at Larkspur must. He can be very . . ." She sighed, her breath ragged.

"He can be very *what*?"

Connie lowered her voice. "He's traveled to the city this week, to visit with his secret club. Mother never would have dared to invite Mrs. Spencer and the five children if Father were around. We're supposed to keep it a secret."

Poppy reached out and grabbed Connie's hands. The girl tried to pull away, but Poppy held tight. "Listen to me," she said, unsure what words might spill out. "You're not safe here. None of you are. Not your mother. Not your brother. And it's all Frederick's fault. Your father is not a good man."

Connie's arms went limp. "What are you talking about?"

"Your mother brought Mrs. Spencer here for a reason. She says that scary things have been happening at Larkspur." Connie nodded, her lips trembling. "You need to convince your mother to take you away. Maybe on a short trip down to the city. *Anywhere* but here."

"But why? What did Father do?"

Poppy sifted through all the thoughts swirling through her mind. The spirits of Larkspur had sent her into this vision for a reason. What was it? Could she change things? Or maybe find out—

That was it! "He's made a deal," Poppy said. "Signed a pact."

"What kind of deal? For a new painting?"

Not really, thought Poppy.

"Never mind. Where would he keep this . . . this *deal*?"

Connie tilted her head. "Maybe his art studio? He's always there, with his paints, and it's the only room in the house that he won't allow the staff to—"

The house jolted. The floorboards shuddered, and cracking sounds raced along the ceiling.

The thing that Frederick Caldwell had made a deal with had finally sensed that Poppy and the others were here, trying to change its history.

Suddenly, the great mirror slid off the wall and dropped to the ground beside the girls. They grabbed at each other, cringing as the top of the frame began to tilt toward them. But then Connie cried, "Help me!" and reached up to catch the mirror. Poppy shoved at her own reflection. The glass shattered on her palms, sharp pain slicing across her skin as the mirror broke into pieces, the frame falling around the two girls like a hoop, crashing to the floor.

Connie took Poppy's hand and tugged, swinging her around the nearest corner. Poppy's palm stung like nothing she'd ever felt before. "This way," Connie said.

Poppy took two steps before someone slammed into her. She fell backward, losing Connie's grip and banging her head against the hard wooden floor.

CHAPTER 19

AZUMI SCREAMED AS she saw Dash and Poppy collide. They both dropped.

A girl was standing over them, her pale skin making her frightened eyes enormous. It was Poppy's cousin, Frederick's daughter. Her hands were covered in red and her apron was torn. What had happened?

Poppy groaned as Azumi took her arm. Close up, Azumi noticed that Poppy's face and shirt were speckled with red too.

"Come on!" Connie cried, looking over her shoulder, as if something were about to jump out from around the corner of the hall.

Dash scrambled to his feet, still clutching the bolt cutter he'd taken from the barn's loft.

"You almost impaled me with that!" Poppy shouted at him.

"We were trying to find you!" he answered. "You left us alone in that room with those strange kids."

Only then did he seem to notice Connie standing with them, panting, panicked. He raised an eyebrow in recognition. Strange how it seemed nothing could surprise him anymore.

Connie waved them down the hall a few more steps.

"The house shook," said Azumi, following. "And then the music box flew off the table. The lid slammed shut and the tune stopped playing, and then—"

"The candles blew out," said Dash. "Everyone was shouting, knocking chairs over, bumping into one another as they tried to run."

"The house found a way to stop the music," said Poppy. "Maybe it was the only thing protecting us."

"*The house?*" Connie asked them, shaking her head. "I don't understand."

"We have to get out of here," Azumi said.

"And go where?" asked Dash. "We're literally standing inside the monster."

"*The monster?*" Tears streaked Connie's cheeks. She turned to Poppy. "I don't know what to do. Help me!"

Poppy's face grew serious. "We're taking you with us. What's the quickest way out of the house?"

Connie took a deep breath and then nodded at the closest door. "Through here."

The four of them ran, the floor trembling, the walls rattling. Frederick Caldwell's paintings fell from their hooks, as if chasing them down the hall.

The faster the group sprinted, the louder the commotion grew behind them. Azumi was afraid to look back. It sounded like something was tearing the house apart, piece by piece, and devouring it.

Connie brought them around another bend in the corridor, but they met a wall instead of an exit. A dead end. They turned back and then pressed themselves against one another, as if ready to fight whatever was chasing them.

The shaking in the hall grew stronger, so strong that Azumi's vision began to vibrate. It was worse than any earthquake she'd experienced on the West Coast or while in Japan. Everything blurred.

Then something even stranger happened. The ceiling lifted away. The floorboards parted and broke. The walls splintered and flew off into whirling shadows. Connie was screaming, as if trying to wake herself from a nightmare, and Poppy clung to her.

Azumi felt a pang of jealousy, wishing for her sister's touch.

Darkness rushed forward, embracing them and bursting through their bodies, pushing apart their cells, disintegrating them from the inside out.

CHAPTER 20

DASH AND DYLAN are hiding in a corner of the Hollywood studio, away from the glare of the hot set lights. The cast and crew mill about, ignoring them. The brothers play a game, tossing Skittles at each other, only they're laughing so hard that they miss most of them.

Chewing on a candy, Dylan says, "Everyone's looking at us like we have two heads."

"It's all your imagination," says Dash, rolling his eyes. "Stop being weird."

Dylan stops smiling. He leans close. "You don't *really* think I'm weird, do you, little brother?"

Dash feels his face heat up. He hates it when Dylan calls him that. But Dylan won't cut it out. Ever. "Well, yeah," says Dash. "You're weirder than me, for sure."

Dylan's eyes grow dark. "You'd never leave me alone here, would you?"

Dash shakes his head, confused. "What are you talking about?" Something in his hand feels suddenly heavy. He glances down and sees that he's clutching a metal tool with sharp blades at the tip. He looks up to find his brother standing only inches away from him now, eyes glaring—or pleading—suddenly watery. "Okay, okay, geez . . . I'll never leave you alone! Not here. Not anywhere."

Dylan grins, and Dash feels chills tickle his lower back. "Promise," Dylan says.

The set has changed around them. It no longer looks like a living room in the suburbs, but instead, like a dusty shed.

How did we get here? Dash wonders.

The lights blink out, and the set is thrown into darkness.

Never leave . . .

"*Promise!*" But Dylan no longer looks like Dylan. He looks like a clown, with a white plastic face, a red gash of a frown, and two black pits for eyes.

Before Dash can answer, Dylan has wrapped his fingers around Dash's throat. He's squeezing. Squeezing. Dash's eyes water. He can't catch his breath or move his hands. Something is trying to pull him to the ground.

"*Promise!*" the clown hisses again.

But Dash can't—

"Dash!" someone shouts in his ear. "The bolt cutter!"

And Dash swings his hands upward, feeling the hard connection as the bolt cutter smashes into Dylan's chest. He tumbles backward, groaning in shock.

Air rushes into Dash's lungs, and he collapses against the door of the burned-out car. Poppy and Azumi appear at his side. And reality crashes in around him.

Azumi didn't have more than a second after being torn from the vision before she saw that the Specials had arrived. She was leaning over Dash when Matilda, Irving, and Dylan came back.

Poppy rolled to the floor, slipping away from Matilda's outstretched arms. Azumi ducked around the side of the car to avoid Irving. But Dylan tackled Dash. The boys flailed in the dirt and the mud.

Azumi called out, "Dylan, leave him alone!" Irving wheeled around the car after her. She shifted her weight to avoid him and immediately lost sight of the twins. "Poppy, help him!"

From the other side of the car, Poppy cried out in frustration. Matilda was crouching, about to leap toward her. At the last second, Poppy raised her foot and steadied her leg, and the sole of her sneaker smashed into Matilda's chest. Kicking out, Poppy knocked the girl to the ground. Without thinking, she turned over and then scrambled toward the bolt cutter, which Dash had dropped. The boys continued to struggle, Dash groaning under the weight of his twin. Poppy swung the heavy tool at Dylan. It almost hurt to listen as the bladed tip swiped at Dylan's shoulder. Distracted, Dylan turned to her and snarled.

A weight dropped onto Poppy's back. Matilda yanked at her hair and pulled her head backward. The cat mask stared down at Poppy, only inches away. She could feel Matilda's breath on her forehead, puffing through the small slit in the plastic. She swung out her arms, trying to find the bolt cutter, but it had fallen somewhere out of reach.

Matilda jerked Poppy's head so hard, Poppy heard a crack. Pain shot down her spine and panic flooded her veins. It was the first time that Poppy feared that Matilda no longer only wished to scare her . . . or even hurt her. The girl was actually trying to kill her—to pop her skull off her neck, like a piece of fruit from a tree branch . . .

"Help me!" Poppy screamed.

Dash heard her cry out but he couldn't reach her, not with Dylan clinging to his side. Poppy's swing of the bolt cutter had knocked Dylan askew, and Dash had turned over and crawled toward the car. Despite the flat tire and rotted carriage, there were still several inches of space beneath it.

With another flash from the sky outside, Dash could see that the bolt cutter was only about a foot away. He grabbed it and then scrambled forward. Dylan lost his grip as Dash forced himself under the car. Pressed to the sour-smelling dirt, he felt a little safer. If he didn't catch his breath soon, he wouldn't be able to go on.

Under the car, he began to approach Poppy and Matilda from a different angle. Poppy cried out as Matilda pulled her head back again.

Dylan reached toward Dash, swinging his arm back and forth, but Dash darted out of the way. "Azumi!" he called out. "Do something!"

Dash heard footfalls to his left. They were headed around the front of the car, toward where Matilda was gripping Poppy.

But another pair of feet followed close behind. These were linked by a short length of rusted chain. Irving!

Dash used the last of his strength to push himself forward. He shoved the bolt cutter out from under the car, the tip of it catching the chain, and Irving fell forward, slamming to the ground.

The bear mask turned to look at him, snarling deep and low. Dash was paralyzed with fear. He could hear Dylan scurrying toward him from the back of the car. If Irving came at him from the front, there would be no escape. Irving's chain rang out as he tried to shake the bolt cutter away.

Azumi stood frozen as Poppy squealed in agony.

An idea struck Dash like a blow to the temple. He wiggled forward quickly and then grasped both handles of the tool. Irving's bear mask seemed to smirk before its plastic mouth opened wide, rank breath pouring out of a deep hole.

Dash squeezed the bolt cutter shut, the blades closing on the rusted links of Irving's chain. Before Dash could blink, the chain snapped.

The bear's jaws closed, and a gasp came from inside the mask. Seconds later, a long, thin crack appeared in the center of the bear's head. The crack spread, crumbling faster and faster, as the mask fell apart.

Matilda and Dylan screamed as if in pain.

Glancing back, Dash watched Dylan pull himself out from under the car. Matilda fell off Poppy and scrambled away from her, focused on Irving. Poppy clutched at her neck. "You okay?" Azumi asked.

Poppy groaned. "Just keep her away from me . . ." Azumi rushed over, helping her sit up, watching Matilda and Dylan in case they came at them again.

Dash stared at the boy who'd been chained up like a circus animal for decades. His brown eyes were barely visible, but Dash could see tears glistening. Irving reached toward Dash, and Dash allowed the boy to take his hands and pull him from the wreck's undercarriage.

Crouching beside him, Dash managed to ask, "Are you . . . *you?*"

Irving touched his own face, then smiled and nodded.

"I didn't take off your mask," said Dash. "How—" But before Dash could finish, Irving began to fade, his skin growing translucent.

"You gave me what I needed," said Irving, his voice soft, as if coming from a distant room, "what Cyrus took from me . . . my freedom . . . Thank you . . ."

Then he too was gone. Just like Randolph and Esme and Aloysius. All that was left were the links that had enclosed his ankles. He'd never wear them again.

A scuffling sound made Dash stiffen.

Matilda and Dylan were standing side by side, several feet from where Azumi sat with Poppy, the expressions on their masks even more exaggerated than before, eyebrows tilted downward, their smiles full of teeth.

"Over here," Dash whispered to the two girls. "Hurry."

Poppy held her neck tenderly. Azumi slid backward along the ground, wrapping an arm around Poppy's waist, pulling her along. But for every move the girls made, Matilda and Dylan took a threatening step forward.

CHAPTER 21

POPPY AND AZUMI edged around to the front of the car, where Dash had managed to stand up, Matilda and Dylan on their heels.

The air crackled with static. Dash felt the hairs on his arms rise, and it wasn't from goose bumps this time. "Get down!" he whispered, pushing the girls to the ground as a pinkish-white light filled the shed.

The explosion was so deafening, it erased their screams.

It rang in Dash's eardrums as he looked up to see a new hole in the ceiling. Bits of wood rained down from the spot where lightning had struck. A small chunk smacked him in the forehead, but he barely noticed. Blue light was flickering nearby, and a crackling hum filled the space.

Poppy gasped as she pushed herself up, and Azumi pointed past Dash's shoulder. He turned and saw a group of children surrounding Matilda and Dylan, holding hands, enclosing the two in what looked like a game of ring-around-the-rosy. But these weren't ordinary children. They appeared to be made of electricity, their bodies pulsing with light, strings of sparks snapping between each of them like a Tesla coil.

Azumi stammered, "Who— Who are they?"

In the center of the circle, Matilda and Dylan broke apart and ran at the spectral children, trying to smash through the barricade, but when they approached the edge, the static snapped at them, flinging them backward. The children stepped forward, shrinking the circle.

"Whoever they are," said Dash, "they're helping us."

Azumi stood frozen. She knew it was Dylan who'd just flown backward, but all she could see was Marcus arcing through the air, over and over and over. She'd trusted the thing that looked like Moriko. Her fault!

"It's *them*," said Poppy, breathless. "Look!"

Then Dash could see their details. Of the ten, half wore blindfolds and the old-fashioned clothes he'd seen during the vision of the Larkspur séance. He recognized the others as the kids from the Polaroid in the loft. They were helping.

Matilda and Dylan yowled like trapped animals.

Suddenly, all the electric children turned to look at Dash, Azumi, and Poppy. They appeared terrified but hopeful—and then their bodies began to dim. Who knew how much longer they could keep it up?

Dash realized what they wanted. "They're giving us a chance," he said. "Run!"

Grabbing the lantern, he chased Azumi and Poppy toward the open door. He expected it to slam closed, but then the three were outside, the rain drenching them again, and Dash paused and looked back. The circle of blue light had shrunk further. Strings of electricity licked at the two at the center, and Matilda and Dylan shrieked in anger and pain. Dash could almost feel the buzzing in his own skin, burning hot. Like the lamp that had electrocuted Dylan back in the dressing room.

Your fault!

He shook his head, trying to contain a flood of tears.

His brother called out to him from within the spectral prison, his voice pleading, desperate. "Don't leave me here!"

Promise, Dash . . .

PROMISE!

"That's not your brother talking," said Poppy, slipping her hand into his own. "Come on. We don't have much time." And she yanked him away from the doorway.

CHAPTER 22

THE THREE RAN across the meadow. With every step, every jounce, every leap through the tall, wet grass, Poppy's neck and spine prickled with sharp pain, and she grew more and more aware of how close Matilda had come to seriously hurting her.

Beside her, Azumi muttered to herself. And Dash . . . Dash was bawling. He was trying to keep quiet, but Poppy could hear him, even though the wind whipped at them and the trees creaked and cracked in the forest to their right.

Poppy focused on the ground just ahead. She knew that the house was still up the hill to the left. They were keeping their distance.

"This is it!" Azumi shrieked when they stumbled out of the tall grass and onto the gravel of the driveway. "Our way out!"

"Don't jinx this," said Dash, his voice ragged.

Poppy grabbed her friends and hugged them close. "We did it!" she yelled, not caring who or what heard her. She wanted to throw her joy into the house's face . . . if the house *had* a face.

Larkspur was a place of pain. Of death.

It was the beginning of every bad thing that had ever happened to her—the reason her mother had left, the reason the girls at the group home called her crazy, the reason she'd always felt so isolated and alone.

Her own face burned as she thought about how she'd abandoned Connie in the house as the darkness had swallowed them up. Connie had never made it out—not in the vision, and not during the fire that would devour the nursery a month after the séance.

She knew she couldn't change the past, and yet . . .

If Poppy hadn't opened the door to the wrecked car, she never would have met her cousin. If she had ignored the sound, if she had been a little less brave, maybe the house would never have found her and sent its invitation.

Did I put myself *on Larkspur's radar?* Poppy wondered.

Eventually, the rain stopped and the wind died down. The farther they walked from the house on the hill, the better Poppy felt. And by the time she crossed the line of trees with Azumi and Dash back into the forest toward Hardscrabble Road, Poppy felt resigned. Someday, maybe Poppy could even forget about what had happened here. She'd lose memories about the house and the letter from Delphinia, and maybe—hopefully?—eventually her own mother. Maybe Connie would be kind enough to stop appearing in the mirrors.

What a dream to be able to finally move on—to build a life from what was coming rather than whatever she'd always carried with her.

"It's strange," whispered Dash, ducking under a low-hanging branch.

"What's strange?" asked Azumi, following him farther along the driveway, into the dripping darkness of the woods.

"Look around. Larkspur is letting us leave. After everything we've been through. After all the fighting. We're just walking out."

"The friendlier ghosts are protecting us," said Poppy, thinking of her cousin and the kids in the loft and the blindfolded wards of the veiled spirit medium. "We still have people on our side."

"Dead people, you mean," said Azumi.

"Better than no one at all," Poppy said, surprised at her sudden anger. "They've given up a lot to help us leave."

"But we *haven't* left yet."

Poppy rolled her eyes, heaved a breath, and kept walking.

CHAPTER 23

EVEN THOUGH AZUMI walked between Poppy and Dash, far from the branches at the edges of the driveway, she felt more terrified than ever. Being back in the woods near the gate should have made her relieved. They were close to the exit of these wretched grounds, and they were only getting closer. To safety, to her parents, to *home*.

But the voices in her head were growing louder, more persistent. And what if they followed her past Larkspur's gate?

Leave the path . . . Get out . . . Run . . .

Run? But to where?

What if she made it all the way back to Washington, only to find herself sleepwalking again—still haunted by the forest where Moriko had disappeared? Could she ever tell her parents what had happened to her here? Would they believe her? Could

Azumi believe herself anymore? What if she was broken now, just like Cyrus's Specials? What could she do to release herself, like they'd done for the ghosts of Larkspur?

And how could she ever *leave the path* when the path kept popping up underneath her feet?

A dozen yards ahead, the stone wall appeared. Yes! This was the spot where the driver had dropped her off early that morning—a lifetime ago. Only a few more steps and they'd all be free.

But then Azumi noticed Dash and Poppy slowing down. "What's wrong?" she asked.

Dash raised the lantern, and Azumi finally saw. The driveway led up to the wall itself. The gate was gone.

"We must have gone the wrong way," said Azumi, glancing off into the shadows on either side of the trail.

"You know that's not true," said Dash, shivering. "There was one way in. And one way out. And it was right here, at the driveway. No wonder the house let us just keep walking. We can't leave!"

"Says who?" Poppy asked, rubbing her neck. "Don't tell me you've never climbed a wall before," she teased with a small smile.

Dash's lip quivered. "But Dylan . . ." He glanced over his shoulder, as if his brother might have somehow managed to follow him this far. "How can I leave him here?"

Poppy looked at Azumi for help.

"Come on, Dash," said Azumi, walking toward the dead end, feeling very small at the front of the group. "We have to try. Who's first?"

They decided to boost Dash, so he'd be able to help them climb up. Poppy and Azumi joined hands and bent down to form a step, then they counted to three and catapulted him upward. He caught some thick vines near the top of the wall, and with a few grunts, managed to pull himself up to the lip. Azumi watched, her hands squeezed into tight fists, as Dash scrambled, swinging one knee over the top. He sat for a second, staring out at what neither girl could see. "No!" he cried. "No! Please, no!"

CHAPTER 24

THE WORLD TILTED, and Dash clutched at the stones beneath him. Overhead, the clouds were breaking up, starlight illuminating the area.

"What's wrong?" Poppy called out, already reaching for handholds to climb up.

"What do you see?" asked Azumi.

Dash glanced down. How could he explain what he was looking at? Just below, where Hardscrabble Road should have been running parallel to the wall, there was only more driveway stretching forward into more forest. And from this height, Dash could see into the distance over the tops of the trees. Rising into the night sky was Larkspur's tallest tower.

That was impossible! The house was *behind* them. He was certain of it.

But when he glanced back the way they'd come, he noticed the same view. The same tower, rising over the same trees.

It was like he was sitting on the edge of a giant double mirror—Larkspur ahead, Larkspur behind—and he was stuck between the two.

"I-I'm not sure," he called to the girls. He couldn't trust his eyes, and he didn't wish to scare them more.

Poppy took the lantern from Azumi and handed it up to Dash to hold while they both climbed. After a short struggle, Poppy and Azumi sat beside him, their mouths agape.

"So then I'm *not* imagining this?" he asked. They shook their heads, speechless.

The only difference between the two houses was that the one on the hill ahead of them was lit up—all the windows shining, as if to say *Come in*—while the one behind them was dark. Dead.

Laughter echoed through the trees at their backs like a brief burst of wind. Dash could almost feel it run up his spine, cruel fingers scratching him. "You think this is funny?" he screamed at the night. "You won't be laughing soon!"

"Shh, Dash!" whispered Azumi. "You're going to make it mad."

"I don't care. It's making me mad. You hear me?! *MAD!*" Dash screamed again, rage tearing into the night, waking birds from nearby branches.

"Be quiet, please!" Poppy pleaded.

Dash spun on her with such force he nearly fell off the wall. "You don't get to tell me what to do!"

Poppy's eyes went wide. Her lips parted as if she wanted to answer but was suddenly afraid.

"This is *your* fault!" he yelled, glaring at her. "All of this! Me and Azumi have been following you all day long. We trusted you. And you listened to what we had to say. But then you just . . . stopped. You've gotten us trapped over and over! The games tent. The mirror maze. The loft in the stable. The séance. We agreed that we need to stick together. But I guess you think that doesn't apply to you."

"I was only doing what I thought would help," Poppy whispered.

"Help *you*," Dash said. "And the people that you wanted to help. You're obsessed with the Specials. You've got plans out the wazoo to make sure *they* get out of this horrible place, but where's your plan for Dylan? Huh? How come you don't care about him?"

"I do," said Poppy. "But after everything we've seen Dylan do, I had to agree with *you* that leaving him was for the best. He attacked you, Dash!"

"You're not hearing me." Dash's face grew grim. "I'm done," he said calmly. "I'm not following you anymore."

"You guys!" Azumi whimpered. "This is not a good idea. We need one another."

127

"Tell that to Poppy," he said.

Poppy's eyes glistened in the starlight. Her face was a mask of shock.

"I'm not blindly trusting her instincts, especially when her instincts don't include rescuing what's important to the rest of us."

"So what am I supposed to do?" asked Azumi.

Dash blinked. He felt hollow. "Save yourself."

The wall shook, wavering back and forth as if it weren't quite solid. Dash scrambled to hold on, but the stones seemed to shift away from his grip, and the lantern slipped from his hands. Glass shattered below. He tumbled forward, the ground rushing quickly to meet him. Stage combat lessons with Dylan blinked through his brain, and Dash remembered to roll into the fall. Still, the world spun as he hit the driveway with enough force to knock his breath away, the girls landing on either side of him.

Wham! Crunch!

Then, silence.

CHAPTER 25

POPPY SAT UP slowly, surprised that her body didn't hurt more. Dash's phone was lying in the brush several feet away, its pale light illuminating the immediate surroundings, and the lantern was on its side, the glass cage cracked. Dash grabbed both.

The spot where they'd landed looked like the place where they'd climbed up. But they were on the other side of the wall now.

Poppy whispered as if to herself, "All the king's horses and all the king's men couldn't put Poppy together again."

Dash's eyes darted toward her. "This isn't a joke."

Poppy's face flushed. "I'm not making a joke."

Dash rose to his feet, shaking. "We have to go back."

"What?" said Azumi. "Why?"

"There's got to be a different way out."

Poppy sighed. "Are you sure you're not just scared for your brother?"

"Of course I'm scared for my brother! But I'm also worried that we're going to be trapped here, like, forever!"

Azumi whimpered. "The creature is back there. Didn't you hear it coming for us?"

As if in answer, a howl screamed out from the other side of the wall.

The three of them bolted farther up the driveway toward the new version of the house all aglow at the top of the hill. Dash paused and looked back the way they'd come.

Azumi went on, "I can't look at that thing again, Dash."

"There's got to be something we can do," said Poppy. "Here. On this side of the wall. What if we . . ." She was quiet for a moment. "What if we try and finish what we started? Free the last of the Specials? Matilda."

"But this isn't just about the Specials anymore," said Dash. "This is about . . . the painter. Frederick Caldwell. We can do something about his pact." He lowered his voice. "The deal that he made with the shadow creature. We destroy it. We end the pact, we end its power over us . . . over *everything* that's trapped in this place. *That's* our escape."

130

"The pact," said Poppy. "Connie said her father wouldn't let anyone into his studio. I bet you the pact is in there!"

"But that would mean we have to go into the house," said Azumi. "I'd rather take my chances out here."

"Those chances aren't very good," said Poppy. "Outside is just as dangerous as inside. Dash is right. To end this, we *have* to go back in. We have to find the studio."

"No, we don't," said Dash.

Poppy's mouth dropped open. "You have another idea?"

Dash nodded. "We burn it. We burn it all to the ground."

"I think I like this idea," said Azumi.

"It won't matter where the studio is," said Dash. "Frederick's pact will go up in flames with the rest of Larkspur."

"But fires haven't stopped the house before," said Poppy.

"I'm doing this," Dash answered. "Someone else should get a say, right, Azumi?"

Azumi crossed her arms over her stomach and narrowed her eyes at the ground. She thought Dash might be right—burning the house was like getting off the path, right?—but there were no sides now. *Save yourself*, he'd said. Maybe they were just three strangers now, stuck together until they found a way out. Or until the house trapped them there for good.

CHAPTER 26

COMING AROUND THE bend in the driveway, they saw lights in the distance—Larkspur House on the hill. With windows glowing, it appeared to be watching for its next battle.

Azumi wrung her hands. "It's expecting us."

"Of course it's expecting us," said Dash. "But is it expecting *this*?" He held up the lantern.

Poppy scoffed. "Maybe that's what it wants."

"You think it *wants* us to try and burn it down?" asked Azumi.

Poppy nodded, smiling sadly. "I think it wants us to *try*."

"Great," said Dash, swallowing down the last of the gritty taste that was coating his tongue. "I'm happy to give it what it wants."

He turned to face the house, lifting his chin to show that its tricks hadn't broken him. As if in answer, all the lights in the windows went out, leaving the trio suddenly exposed in the darkness of the meadow, the flame in Dash's grip like a blip on a radar. He released a slow breath and then continued up the hill, Larkspur now a massive shadow with hundreds of black, glassy eyes reflecting starlight.

The three walked toward the closest corner of the house—a wooden wall covered in vines, purple flowers budding and straining toward the night sky.

"Well, here we are," said Dash, holding up the lantern. "This is it." He turned a latch in the lantern's glass cage, opening a small door.

"Go ahead," said Poppy flatly.

Who's laughing now? Dash thought, reaching out and breaking off a long piece of the flowering vine. He held the stick into the flame and watched as its tip quickly caught fire. But when he brought the fire out of the lantern and held it toward the wooden slats on the side of the building, the night air seemed to pinch the light away. It fizzled with a hiss, smoke rising from the end of the stick.

Dash felt his cheeks flush. He tried again. And again the flame went out before he could get it within inches of Larkspur's siding.

What's wrong, little brother?

Dash flinched away from the wall. "Dylan?" he called out.

Azumi touched his shoulder. "Dylan's not here, Dash," she whispered gently.

You don't really want to destroy Larkspur, do you? If you leave, I stay behind.

"Stop it," Dash said, shaking his head. "You're not real."

Oh, I'm real, said Dylan's voice. *As real as you.*

Dash could feel the girls staring at each other with concern. Ignoring them, he gripped the nozzle at the base of the lantern. He unscrewed the cap until it fell to the grass, and the dizzying smell of kerosene wafted out of the container, making his eyes water. He splashed the liquid out of the lantern and onto the creeping vines. "Let's hope this works," he said, lighting another twig and then holding it out. This time, the fire bloomed and spread quickly, chasing the flammable liquid up the wall.

Poppy gasped at the sudden heat and light. Azumi stepped back, wide-eyed with surprise.

Triumphant, Dash almost began to laugh. But he was suddenly overcome with memories. Dylan coming through the doorway of the dressing room. The bucket tumbling from the top of the door. The water drenching him. Dylan reaching for the sparking lamp.

You're killing me all over again, said Dylan's voice in his head. *You hate me! You've always hated me!*

"That's not true!" Dash shouted, stepping back, taking in the blaze. "It was an accident! I never meant to—"

The fire began to diminish, smoke rising thick and white from the green vines and purple flowers, as if the house itself were putting it out.

"*Nooo!*" Dash wailed, clutching at his head.

"But it was working!" said Azumi.

Poppy spoke up. "Dash—"

He cut her off. "Don't say a word. Please."

The fire fizzled away. Enraged, Dash swung the lantern, its glow flickering wildly inside the glass cage, and then threw it as hard as he could at the house. The glass exploded, squirting flame and fuel in every direction. The girls leapt away, pulling Dash with them as they fell to the ground several feet from the new blaze.

Dash bit his lip. Hoping. Hoping. Then the fire went out again.

Dylan's voice began to chuckle inside his head. *Nice try . . . little brother.*

"Shut up, Dylan! I'm trying to help you!"

The voice went silent. This hurt worse than the teasing.

"Dylan? I'm sorry. Are you here?"

"Dash, who are you talking to?" Poppy asked. "We're the only ones here."

"What do we do now?" asked Azumi.

"What I suggested," said Poppy, her voice firm. "We need to go back into the house and find Frederick's studio. His pact has got to be there."

CHAPTER 27

THEY LEFT THE mess of glass behind and started searching for an open door or window. But every entry they came to was sealed shut, the glass unbreakable. It was as if Larkspur knew what they were trying to do and wouldn't allow them back inside. This only proved to Poppy that they were on the right track.

"Come on, Connie," Poppy whispered as they strolled along the edge of the house. "Let us in."

"Who are *you* talking to, Poppy?" asked Dash. "Maybe she's not here anymore either."

Poppy pressed her lips together, refusing to look at him. "Connie?" she yelled out. "Please!"

Frustrated, Dash slammed his foot against the foundation. Jumping back, he watched a pile of large stones spill onto the ground, crushing the tall grass right in front of him. The stones had left a wide hole in the foundation.

"What was that, Dash?" asked Azumi.

"I didn't mean to."

A stale stench wafted into Poppy's face when she leaned down, and she coughed. It smelled like something gone rotten in a warm refrigerator. It smelled familiar.

"This was not the way in I was hoping for," said Azumi.

Dash shook his head, glancing back down the hill, as if he were about to run.

Poppy shrugged, trying to shake off a cloud of panic. "What other choice do we have?"

"This is what the house wants," said Dash, taking a step backward.

Poppy lowered her voice. "But it's what *we* want too." She crouched on her hands and knees and brought her face up to the opening. "How about some light, Dash?"

He pulled his phone from his pocket and shone the flashlight through the crevice. "What if the house just puts walls around us to keep us from finding the pact?" he asked.

There appeared to be a slight drop onto a bit of crumbled foundation inside the wall. And beyond that, a sea of impenetrable pitch.

"That won't happen," said Poppy. "Remember what Cyrus

wrote about hope and fear? How, when they're intertwined, they make us feel alive? If you remove one, you can't have the other." Dash and Azumi stared at her, confused. "Well, if Larkspur is 'alive,' it's gotta work the same way. If it locks us up within its walls, it eliminates its worry, its *fear*, that we'll beat it. And without that, the house has no *need* to go on. It needs us— all of us—to play its game. Right up until the very end, when it thinks it's finally the winner. And that's when we'll destroy its desire to hurt anyone ever again. No more hope . . . but no more fear either. We'll turn this place into an empty shell, just like it's tried to do to us. *I promise*." Her eyes began to sting. "Dash, I won't ask you to follow me again. But I really hope you choose to." Before the tears could fall, Poppy slid her legs forward and climbed in.

After a few seconds, Azumi's voice echoed behind her. "Everything all right?"

"So far," said Poppy, turning back and raising a hand to help her friend through the gap. When Azumi took her palm, Poppy's skin screamed out, reminding her of the cuts from the broken mirror. Poppy winced and held her hand to her chest until it stopped throbbing.

Dash grunted as he followed behind Azumi, shimmying onto the pile of broken foundation and bringing the light into the space. Poppy smiled at him, but he wouldn't look at her.

Instead, he held up his phone. Black brick walls, coated in dust, loomed like they wanted to squeeze them all together. A thin hallway stretched off into the distance. Large spiders skittered away from Dash's light, searching for cracks to hide in. The dark dirt floor beyond the foundation looked well worn, as if people had walked this path over and over.

Azumi's ankle twisted as the foundation gave way, and she fell into Poppy's arms. Glancing down, she screamed. She hadn't been standing on a rock or a brick, but a skull. A small, bleached human skull. The girls scurried farther into the narrow hallway while Dash stared at the pile of bones that was mixed in with the rubble.

"Let's go," Poppy whispered. "Before the house starts to mess with us."

"It's already started," said Dash flatly.

They gathered together and walked slowly through the skinny passage, listening for sounds in the dark. Ahead, the flashlight glinted off one of the walls. There was a small copper plaque that had been screwed into the black brick. Something was engraved on it.

Consolida Caldwell.

Ice flooded Poppy's spine.

"Why's your cousin's name posted down here?" Azumi asked.

Poppy ran her fingers along the wall. She had a sense of what was behind the bricks, but she was too frightened to say it.

Several feet farther down the corridor was another copper tag. This one read: *Eugenia Caldwell*.

"Connie's mother," said Poppy.

On the next tag was *Frederick Caldwell*. The painter who'd made the pact with the shadow creature.

"I don't understand," said Dash. "What kind of game is the house playing now?"

"I don't know," said Poppy, her voice shaking.

They came to more copper plates. More names.

Gage Vogel.

Sybil Simonov.

Eliza Turner.

James Han.

Orion Robideaux.

She refused to tell Dash and Azumi that these were Cyrus's first orphans—the ones who had drowned during a boat accident on the Hudson River in the thirties. She didn't want to scare them.

A quiet hum murmured through the passages. Poppy tried to walk more quickly, but Dash and Azumi kept slowing, and she didn't dare ask Dash to keep up. He read out more names. Some seemed familiar, but others were not.

Javier & Philip Zullo.

Angelo & Beryl Fox.

Verity Reese.

Saul Barron.

"Didn't Cyrus write something about Larkspur having a crypt?" asked Dash, stepping over to the center of the corridor.

Azumi blanched, pulling her fingertips away from one of the markers.

They came to a section of red brick that looked newer than the rest, like a doorway that had been recently sealed. A few feet beyond this patch, four other dark openings appeared to be waiting for the same treatment. Dash shone his light inside the first.

It was small, no bigger than the square-shaped closet that Poppy had shared with Ashley back at Thursday's Hope.

While Azumi and Dash peered into the other spaces, Poppy noticed the name on the copper tag screwed into the new brick in front of her. Her jaw dropped, and she gasped, falling back before catching herself on the opposite wall.

"What is it?" asked Azumi. "What's wrong?"

Poppy could only point. She closed her eyes when Dash and Azumi cried out in shock.

The name carved into the shining metal plaque was *Marcus Geller.*

CHAPTER 28

MARCUS IS DEAD because of you, Azumi, just like Moriko this is all your fault your fault your fault this is YOUR FAULT YOUR—

Azumi bit down on her tongue, tearing her gaze away from the marking on the wall. She choked out a sob as she stood closer to the others.

"Is Marcus *in* there?" Dash asked, his voice reverberating throughout the passage.

Poppy shook her head. "It's all part of the game. The house want us to—"

A pounding came from the wall with Marcus's name. The three yelped and then clung to one another, watching as dust rained from the arched stone ceiling.

After a moment, Azumi cried out, "He's alive! We have to

get him out of there!" She stepped toward the plaque, but Poppy yanked on the back of her denim jacket, holding her still.

Boom, boom, boom!

"That's not him," Poppy whispered. "We need to keep moving."

Azumi's eyes grew in surprise. "But what if—"

"Poppy's right," said Dash. "We all saw what the creature did to him. Marcus wasn't breathing when we left him."

"Well, then, maybe we shouldn't have left him!" Azumi cried out. "Maybe we should have stayed with him till he woke up! The creature must have brought him here while we were wandering around outside." She focused on the wall, on his name. "Marcus!" she called out. "Marcus! Can you hear me?!" The pounding was faster now. *Boom, boom, boom!*

She glanced at Poppy and Dash. "I think that means yes. We've got to find something to smash—"

Dash took her elbow and pulled her away from Marcus's plaque. His force surprised her so much that she didn't even think to fight back. Before she knew it, he'd tugged her past the other four dark openings. Poppy followed a little way behind them.

One, two, three, four. A space for each of the house's most recent guests. It had made room in its crypt for them.

Azumi was breathing quickly. Her lungs felt too small.

YOUR FAULT AZUMI YOUR FAULT

"We have to stay focused," said Dash, releasing her arm.

"No!" Azumi cried out. "I won't believe it. I won't! He's alive! He has to be alive. Because if he's not, that means I helped kill him!"

JUST LIKE YOU KILLED MORIKO

"I want to wake up!" Azumi shrieked. "Please, just let me wake up!"

Poppy closed her arms around Azumi, squeezing her tight. Azumi stiffened, but a second later she slumped into Poppy, suddenly sobbing. The tears flowed, wetting her cheeks, until her skin hurt. Somehow, in Poppy's embrace, the voice in her head went quiet. When Poppy started to pull away, Azumi grabbed her and held on. "Okay," she whispered into Poppy's collarbone. "I'll try to focus. But I need you guys to help me. I . . . I'm not okay."

"None of us are okay," said Poppy.

Azumi looked into her eyes. "I think I might be a little worse than you. I think the house knows it's about to break me too."

Dash rubbed her shoulder. "Azumi, I was in a *psych ward* until a couple days ago. My *dead brother* has been following me around for a month. I can relate. Stay strong. You won't break."

Azumi smiled. She wasn't sure if Dash was trying to be funny, but the whole situation suddenly seemed like a comedy.

Stuff like this wasn't supposed to happen to kids. Kids weren't supposed to know what it felt like to be terrified. That was for the world of grown-ups. Adults always tried so hard to keep scary things away from young people. Maybe if young people were allowed to know what fear felt like, all of this would have been easier. Maybe her nightmares would've gone away. Maybe the sleepwalking would've ended.

"It'll be easier if you two stop arguing," she said. "I feel like the house wants to get me out of the way so it can tear you guys apart. Maybe . . . Maybe we all need to be stronger."

YOUR FAULT YOUR—

She took Poppy's hand. The voice stopped again. And Azumi inhaled a deep breath. The fullest gulp of air she'd taken since stepping foot onto the Larkspur estate. It made her feel calmer, like if she could just hold this group together, she could make this ordeal turn out okay. She suddenly realized that this feeling was something worth fighting for.

CHAPTER 29

THE BLACK CORRIDORS twisted in ways that didn't seem to make sense. Dash could swear that the left turn several steps back should've ended with a wall, yet the passage continued to snake forward—a long rise, a little dip. Every now and again, a sound rang out behind them. It could have been feet shuffling along the dirt floor, or grit falling from the cracks in the ceiling. Whatever the case, Dash used it to keep himself moving, even as the walls seemed to press closer together. Every few feet, they encountered another copper tag with another name. It was as if the entire foundation were filled with bodies.

The girls walked in a short chain behind him as he shone the light ahead, his heart pounding, reminding him of the noise that had been coming from within the bricks with Marcus's name on them.

Ahead, a glow appeared, a bare bulb caged to the wall beside a doorway. As they came closer, Dash felt his throat dry up. An accordion door was pulled shut, the empty shaft inside crisscrossed with shadow.

Poppy's voice shook. "Is that the—"

"Elevator," said Dash. "Sure looks like it."

The elevator door was a dead end.

"That's our way up?" Azumi asked.

"The car's missing," said Dash. "And I don't see any button to call it down to us."

"What if we climb?" said Poppy.

"You know what happened the last time we tried to use this thing," said Dash. "The Specials found us."

"What other choice do we have?" Poppy asked.

"Keep wandering around down here?" said Azumi, shaking her head.

No one knew what to say.

Then, from down the dark passage, another shuffling sound echoed out. A scraping noise followed, like nails scratching against the walls. Coming closer. Closer. Quickly now. Any moment, the shroud of shadows would fall away, revealing—

None of them wished to find out what.

They scrambled toward the elevator door. Poppy and Dash grabbed onto it and threw their weight sideways. The door shimmied and then slid several inches.

"Wide enough," said Poppy, nudging Azumi forward. She glanced over her shoulder at the scraping sound as Dash followed Azumi through the opening. Something was shifting in the shadows. She passed the messenger bag to Dash and then snuck into the shaft. "Now help shut it." She nodded at the corridor. "Hurry."

Dash started to glare, but realized it would only hurt him to slow down. They battered at the door until it finally stood as a barrier between themselves and whatever was out there. Dash handed Poppy her bag and then shone his light into the upper reaches of the elevator shaft.

"It's not as large as I remember," said Poppy.

"It kept changing size and shape," said Dash. "Just like the rest of the house." The walls were made of the same black brick as the twisted corridors outside. There was nothing to hold on to, no bars or cables to climb, only a couple of covered rods that ran vertically into the darkness above.

Poppy held out her arms and touched both sides of the shaft. "But this is good!" She leaned against one wall and raised her foot, pressing against the opposite side. "We can push ourselves up. Like this." She brought up her other foot and then levered her body across the shaft.

"Poppy, be careful," said Azumi, worried.

Poppy ignored her. She used her legs to push herself back upward along the wall, walking each foot forward, rising several inches at a time. "Come on, you guys. Try it."

The thing down the hallway scraped the wall as it continued toward them.

"I feel like a rat in a maze," Dash whispered, pressing himself up onto the wall beside Poppy. He carried his phone in one hand, bending his elbow so that its light faced upward. "And the scientist is making sure we do exactly what he wants us to do."

"But you're okay with this, Dash?" Poppy asked.

"Where else can we go?" he answered with a huff.

The group climbed for a few minutes before the brick walls turned to wire mesh. Darkness surrounded the shaft. A closed doorway appeared. "This must be the first floor," said Poppy.

"Shouldn't we just get out?" asked Dash. "We can find our way to the studio through the rest of the house."

"If it lets us," said Azumi.

The accordion gate rattled below them, as if something were testing out the strength of its bars.

"Keep going," said Poppy, staring up the shaft.

"I'm getting out at the next doorway," Dash said through his teeth. "Follow me or not. I don't care."

"We'll follow you, Dash," Poppy answered back.

The group had made it about halfway toward the next door, nearly thirty feet from the bottom of the shaft, when the walls began to vibrate.

"What's that?" Azumi asked. Somewhere nearby, a motor was humming.

Dash focused the flashlight on the metal rods bolted to the wall.

A gear shifted. Metal squealed against metal.

Poppy looked up. "It's the elevator!" she cried out. "Someone's sending it down to us!"

CHAPTER 30

"THE NEXT DOOR is closer." Dash shimmied himself higher. "Come on, you two!"

Poppy couldn't move. Her feet were going numb. The metal rods running up the walls were starting to rattle, and high above her head, a dim glow shone from the car's lamp.

Azumi climbed past Poppy and tugged on the strap of her bag. Poppy was jolted back into her body. She followed the others, pressing her soles against the wall and shifting her spine like a snake.

The rattling grew stronger. The smell of grease stung their noses.

Holding steady, Dash was already at work trying to slide the door open. Azumi waited beside him, staring, horrified, up at the car coming down. "Hurry, Dash!"

Poppy's foot slipped and she slid several inches back down the shaft. The strap of her messenger bag snapped, and Poppy reached down lightning fast, her hand closing on something soft. The bag disappeared into the shadows below. To Poppy's surprise, she found that she'd grabbed the doll that Connie had been holding in her vision. The cloth doll she'd slipped into the pocket of her pinafore.

How had it gotten into Poppy's bag?

There was no time! The bottom of the car was only several yards over her head and approaching swiftly.

Crying out, Dash gave the door a shove, and it finally shivered open. He helped Azumi into the house, then held out his hand to Poppy.

"Go!" she shouted, wiggling herself higher. The door was almost in reach. "Don't wait for me!"

Dash swiveled himself around and then grabbed on to the ledge. One leg up, then the other.

The car kept coming. Dash reached down to her, and Poppy went for his hands. Only a couple of feet left. There wasn't time. If Dash didn't retreat, the car would take his arms. Holding herself in place, Poppy shoved him out of the way, then allowed herself to slip down. Maybe there was still time to reach the door below.

But she couldn't move fast enough. The car was on top of her, blocking Dash's flashlight so she could hardly see. She smelled oil. The bottom of the car seemed to race toward her face, and Poppy squeezed her eyes shut, bracing for impact.

Should I let go? she wondered. *Just fall into the depths of the house?*

A deafening scream nearly knocked her over. The voice echoed on and on.

Then everything went quiet.

Poppy waited, every muscle tensed. But nothing happened. Opening her eyes again, she reached up, and her hand hit something hard only inches above her head. The floor of the car.

It had stopped.

The car had stopped!

She was alive!

"Poppy?" Azumi called from somewhere nearby. "Are you there?" Footsteps knocked on the platform just over her. Azumi must have hopped in and flipped the lever.

"I am!" Poppy yelled back, unable to hold in her hysteria. "Get me out of here! Please!"

"Working on it!"

The sound of the shifting gear rang out again. Poppy prayed that Azumi would move the car in the right direction.

A moment later, the floor drew upward away from her, and the gap by the ledge opened again. Poppy didn't wait. She scrambled out of the shaft as quickly as her legs would allow.

Azumi and Dash huddled around her, sobbing and apologizing.

"What are *you* sorry for?" Poppy managed to ask through her tears. "You guys saved my life."

It was as if they hadn't heard her. For the next few seconds, all they said was, "We're sorry . . . so sorry . . . You're okay . . . We're sorry . . ."

It almost seemed to Poppy like they weren't even talking to her. Like they were apologizing to someone else. To Dylan? To Moriko?

She squeezed the doll tightly, thankful she hadn't lost it.

CHAPTER 31

LAMPS FLICKERED TO life all around the room, filling the space with a golden glow.

Poppy gasped, and the others turned to look. Paintings of landscapes and portraits hung on every wall, filling almost every inch of space. Easels stood in several corners. Blank canvases and half-finished works were propped along the walls. The floor was a mishmash of overlapping rugs, frayed and splattered with color. Wooden boxes were sitting all around, stuffed to their brims with dusty pages and long rolled-up papers, ratty at their edges.

"Frederick's studio?" said Dash, shocked back into himself. "But how? *Why?*" He shook his head. "If the house knew this was where we wanted to go, why did it lead us directly here?"

"But it tried really hard to stop us," said Azumi. "The elevator almost crushed Poppy."

"Exactly. *Almost*."

"*Connie*," whispered Poppy, barely hearing the voices of the others. "She's still helping. Maybe she's the one who made sure we found our way through the basement. Maybe she's the one who pointed us to the right door out of the elevator."

"You're suggesting that your dead cousin was the one who sent the car down the shaft," said Dash, aghast.

"*Maybe*." Poppy nodded. "Maybe she knew we'd get out in the right place in time. That we'd be safe in the end."

Dash raised an eyebrow. "So this is the end, is it?"

"Or maybe the house is still trying to kill us," said Azumi. "Maybe finding this room is another fake-out."

Poppy shook her head, a smile growing on her face. "No. This room is what everything was leading toward. Connie is here. I can sense her. Can't you? It's like . . . I was meant to come."

To this room. To Larkspur! This is my *house*, Poppy thought. *Connie and I only need to fix it. End the curse that Frederick started with his pact. And then maybe we can stay. A family . . . at last.*

Azumi and Dash threw each other a worried glance. "Poppy?" Azumi said gently. "Are you all right?"

Poppy blinked. "We need to look around. See if we can find Frederick's papers."

Dash stood and pulled the gate shut over the elevator door. The others moved into the art studio.

The far wall was a row of windows overlooking the meadow and the woods. Overhead, the stars revealed secrets of their endless constellations. Beyond the trees, Poppy could see the river flowing all the way back down to the city. Maybe she wouldn't have to return to Ms. Tate and the group home after all. Her heart swelled with gratitude.

"Are these pictures of Frederick?" Azumi asked, staring up at one wall. The same face stared out from dozens of frames. If you glanced from portrait to portrait, you'd see a young gentleman transform into a grizzled old man—the shy innocence in his eyes fading, replaced with the shine of insanity. In the few paintings near the bottom of the wall, the subject had lost all sense of humanity. His face grew misshapen, colored a vibrant green or purple or red, white light bursting from his eye sockets, his mouth twisted open in a wide gawp. In others, a mess of paint was thick and gobbed on, suggesting that a man was hiding inside layers of a monstrous cocoon. In the final painting, dark smears only hinted that he was watching from the shadows. It was as if, in the decades since the death of his wife and daughter, Frederick had begun painting himself as a monster.

Poppy couldn't look at them. Hatred squelched her stomach. Or maybe she was just hungry. She suddenly realized how dry her mouth was, how badly she wished for a sip of water.

End the curse and drink all the water you want. Everything here belongs to you now.

Was that Connie's voice? Poppy's breath came faster as she took in the rest of the space.

Looking for the painter's pact, Azumi dug through some of the boxes, while Dash rifled through desk drawers.

A tall object beside one of the easels was covered with a familiar-looking dark fabric. In Cyrus's office that morning, Poppy had stayed away from the drapery, frightened of what she'd see underneath it. But now she knew better. She grasped the cloth and yanked it away. There appeared a six-foot-tall, freestanding full-length mirror. Frederick Caldwell must have used it to paint his self-portraits.

And now Poppy would use it to call to her cousin.

"Connie?" She was so nervous that her voice was a mere squeak. "Are you here?" Poppy stared at her own reflection. In the mirror, she could see Dash and Azumi watching intently, anxiously.

A shadow flickered between them.

Dash flinched away from the spot on the floor where it should have been. But outside of the mirror, there was no shadow. Azumi stared at him, perplexed.

"Connie!" Poppy cried out. "I knew you'd come!"

Dash watched as the shadow solidified into a human shape, but it shuddered and twitched, as if it were fighting off some invisible force. Poppy held her palms to the glass as if that might help, but Connie's image continued to flutter and dance. Suddenly, as if smacked by a giant hand, the shadow jerked back toward the wall of Frederick's self-portraits. Poppy shrieked. The shadow fell to the floor, twitching, then shifted back into a standing position. A moment later, the shadow appeared to be knocked toward the elevator. "Leave her alone!" Poppy hit at the mirror glass, as if she could crawl inside to save her cousin.

"We have to do something!" Azumi cried out. The house was fighting them harder now; it must know how close they were to figuring out its darkest, most powerful secret.

"Hold up!" said Dash, rushing over to the desk he'd been exploring. Reaching into the bottom drawer, he removed a small wooden box decorated with swirling carvings. A tiny metal knob stuck out from its side.

Azumi's jaw dropped. "Is that what I think it is?"

Dash turned the knob, and when he couldn't wind it any further, he opened the lid. "Larkspur's Theme" twinkled out, echoing into the studio. The air felt suddenly still, and a quiet comfort settled onto his skin.

Poppy stepped away from the mirror but continued to stare

into it. The others turned to find the image of Connie standing at Poppy's side in the glass. The psychic medium from the vision had been right: the music was protecting her, protecting all of them.

But who knew how long it would last? Larkspur had a habit of smashing things that got in its way.

"Thank goodness you're okay," said Poppy. Connie nodded, but looked as if she were too exhausted to smile. "We need your help. Frederick's pact . . . We need to know where it is. What does it look like?"

Dash had imagined a standard contract, like the ones his parents had signed for *Dad's So Clueless* back in Hollywood. But he knew that whatever Frederick had signed would be different. Spiritually binding. Whatever the painter had done had given him great fame and limitless wealth. But it had also taken his family from him. Had the man known what would happen? Dash suddenly felt all of Frederick's painted eyes staring at him, daring him to ask the question aloud.

Connie opened her mouth as if to speak; then, she reached into her pocket and pulled out what looked like an old scroll of parchment paper.

The pact! thought Dash.

She quickly unrolled it, showing them that the page was blank. She shook her head and then tore the paper in half, dropping it at her feet.

"What do you mean?" asked Poppy, her voice rising, confused. "There *is* no pact?"

Connie held up a finger as if she were playing a game of charades. She approached the glass from her side of the mirror and opened her mouth. She exhaled, fogging up the area in front of her face. She pressed her finger to the glass and drew a shape like a flower. Five petals radiated from a center point. Connie stared at Poppy as the fog faded away.

Poppy shook her head. "I don't understand." Connie dug around in her pocket, then pulled out a thin paintbrush. The tip was as red as blood.

Dash wondered if it *was* blood.

Then she strolled toward one wall of paintings. Using the brush, she pointed at several of them. Poppy shook her head, tears welling in her eyes. "Can't you please just tell me what you mean?"

"Or write it down," said Dash.

Connie shook her head, tears running down her face. She shoved the brush toward her father's landscapes emphatically.

Azumi waved, trying to get their attention. "What if she's saying that the pact is *inside* one of Frederick's paintings?"

Connie fluttered to the mirror glass, nodding frantically.

Dash approached Poppy. "What if Frederick's pact was an image? A symbol." He pointed at the glass where Connie had fogged it. "The symbol that Connie marked here."

Connie jumped up and down, a huge smile blooming.

Poppy screamed in surprise. "He's right?" Connie nodded. Poppy turned and threw her arms around him again, squeezing him tightly. "Thank you, Dash!"

"Don't thank me," he said, struggling for breath. He felt horrible for everything he'd said to her at Larkspur's gate, and her immense hug told him that she felt the same. Could they trust each other again? Listening to the tinkling of the music box, he suddenly felt like they might. "Thank your cousin."

"Which one is it?" Azumi asked, heading toward the wall of paintings that Connie had pointed at. Connie grew somber, shaking her head. "It's not one of these?" Connie shook her head again and then pointed toward a doorway beyond the elevator.

"The pact is not in this room?" Poppy asked.

Connie raised her hands to her pale face. Splaying her fingers, she dragged them from her eyebrows down to her chin, as if indicating tears.

"Don't be sad," said Poppy, making her voice sound extra excited, hopeful. "We're going to be together soon! Forever!"

Dash's face fell. "Forever?" he asked. What did she mean?

But Poppy ignored him, watching Connie make the gesture over and over. Connie pointed at the doorway again.

"Okay, okay," said Poppy. "We'll go look for it now."

Dash couldn't get her words out of his head. "Poppy, what do you mean? Forever?"

She still pretended not to hear him. "What do we do when we find the right painting?" she asked.

"We can use this," said Azumi, reaching into one of the desk drawers and holding up a tin marked TURPENTINE. She grabbed a silver lighter from an ashtray. "And this."

The tune from the music box started to slow, the melody growing sleepy. The air seemed to vibrate all around it, as if with static.

The hair on the back of Dash's neck prickled. He reached for the box so he could wind it up again.

But the box rose into the air, high over his head.

Dash shouted, "Hey!" He climbed onto the desk, but the spring in the contraption had wound down, and the chimes went silent. The wooden box began to wobble. He could practically feel the house's evil sweeping toward him, filling the space that the music had occupied.

The device exploded, wood splinters flying everywhere. He covered his face, sharp debris hitting the backs of his hands. A second later, the mangled motor dropped to the desk at his feet, and high laughter echoed up from the elevator shaft.

CHAPTER 32

THE ACCORDION DOOR squealed open, and two pairs of hands stretched out of the darkness. Matilda and Dylan dragged themselves onto the floor of the studio and jerked forward into the room as if their limbs were attached to marionette strings. Dash jumped off the desk and ran over to the mirror, where Poppy and Azumi huddled together. Behind them, Connie's reflection had blurred again. She'd pressed herself against the other side of the glass, as if trying to reach Poppy.

Matilda and Dylan glided across the floor, their shoes skidding on the worn rugs, their arms reaching, their hands like claws.

Shivering, Poppy stepped toward them. "I've been waiting

for you," she said, trying to sound brave. "You came. Y-you actually came."

The Specials closed the distance quickly, both of them heading toward Poppy. But Poppy stood still, planting her feet.

"Let's go!" Azumi yelled. She reached for Poppy's arm, but then Dash leapt forward, knocking his brother backward.

Dash and Dylan gripped at each other, falling to the floor, cursing and screaming.

And just as Matilda was about to plow into Poppy, Poppy shoved Connie's doll into the cat girl's hands. Matilda's fingers closed on it as if by instinct. She froze, then glanced at the doll, and a second later, a shattering sound filled the air.

Matilda's mask broke into shards and rained to the floor. Her pale eyes lit up blue, as if powered by some magic, and her mouth spread wide, beaming happiness, surprise, and a bit of fear. Clasping the girl who'd chased her relentlessly through Larkspur, Poppy whispered, "You're okay!"

Dylan shoved Dash away with a snarl. He glanced up as if he were expecting to see Matilda tear Poppy apart with her bare hands, but when he realized Matilda was free, his empty eye sockets flashed golden. Then he went limp.

Poppy felt Matilda's body disintegrate, her slight warmth fading into a coolness like the breeze through her bedroom

window on a spring night. She exhaled, relieved. They were all gone. All the Specials were free.

A stabbing pain shot through Poppy's stomach and she hunched over, gagging. They weren't gone. They were all dead. The house had made sure of that. All their pain, their suffering, their nightmares and panic, had fed the creature.

The monster that had cast its long shadow over Poppy's own life.

This had to end. Now.

Poppy turned back to the mirror. But the glass had turned black. Connie had vanished.

Someone grabbed Poppy's shoulder, and she yelped.

Azumi clutched her arms, was waving something in her face, some sort of shiny metal container. "We need to go!"

Dash crawled over to the girls and stood up, groaning.

Dylan was sitting on the floor a few feet away, just staring at them. His painted frown had reversed. Now a smile stretched across the mask so wide and so high, it was nearly level with his glowing golden eyes.

"He knows something we don't," said Dash, trembling helplessly.

A deep voice echoed out from behind the mask. "You can run . . ." It laughed again. Dylan floated to his feet, as if lifted by invisible strings. "I'll give you a head start. But after that, the game is even."

The floor began to shake.

Poppy, Dash, and Azumi took off, racing toward the darkened door beside the elevator shaft.

CHAPTER 33

AS SOON AS Azumi, Dash, and Poppy went through the door, the smoke hit them, thick and swirling. They all crouched down, then scuttled forward on their hands and knees. Ahead was the crackling sound of fire, and heat radiated toward them.

"Where are we going?" shouted Dash, shining his flashlight forward. The glow reflected off the swirls of ash that were trying to choke him.

"Forward!" said Poppy. "There's no other way."

"There has to be!" said Azumi. "After all this, I'm not going to die in a flipping fire!"

"You'd rather be eaten by a giant monster?" asked Dash.

"It would probably be quicker!"

They'd made it about twenty feet when they heard chuckling

behind them. Dylan had appeared in the doorway, watching them crawl.

"Run," said Dash, rising to his feet and covering his mouth with his hands. "Just . . . run!"

As they raced forward, the smoke began to clear. None of them could see Dylan behind them anymore. The hallways stretched long before them.

"Your brother's the least of our worries now," said Poppy. "The house knows we're here to destroy it. And even more important: We know how! It's going to do everything it can to keep us from reaching Frederick's pact. His special painting."

"Which painting are we looking for?" asked Azumi. "The house is filled with so many."

"*The Five-Sided Man!*" said Dash.

"Yes!" said Poppy. "That one was up in the tower. If we can find our way back there, then maybe—"

Azumi screeched as she skidded to a halt. The walls around them had disappeared. A few inches away, the floor was gone too. They were standing at the edge of an endless room filled with darkness. Below, the sound of fire crackled. There was no light. Only abyss and oblivion. The darkness practically shivered with hunger.

"It's over," said Dash, glancing back the way they'd come. "Dylan is heading for us right now."

"It's not over," said Poppy. "Marcus said something earlier today. The house changes shape, right? In that way, it can push us in certain directions. Keep us from going where it doesn't want us to go."

Two amber orbs appeared in the darkness behind them—the glow from inside Dylan's mask. In a few seconds, he'd be upon them.

"Get to the point!" Dash cried out.

"Sorry! It's just . . . We need to head through the scariest places that the house shows to us. That's how we get where we need to go."

The orbs raced forward.

"So then, what now?" asked Azumi.

Poppy turned toward the bottomless abyss. "We jump."

CHAPTER 34

POPPY BEGAN TO FALL.

Azumi screamed out, "Poppy, wait!"

But a moment later, Poppy's feet landed on solid ground. "It's safe!" she called to the others. "There's a floor. Follow me! Hurry!" The bottomless pit had only been an illusion.

Seconds later, the three raced into the darkness, the walls of the hallway appearing ahead once more. But then the floor began to turn, wrenching sideways like the corkscrew of a roller coaster. The lines of the hall all began to curve so that up ahead, the ceiling was where the floor should be. Poppy held her breath as she spiraled around the house, the floor moving upward, her sneakers maintaining contact. She felt like she should fall over. Soon, her head was facing downward, blood rushing into her cheeks. She kept running as the hall began to twist itself tighter and tighter, looping them quicker and quicker.

"I'm gonna be sick," said Azumi.

"Don't puke on me!" Dash shouted.

"A little puke isn't that big a deal . . . ," Poppy answered. The spinning was too much. She started to feel faint.

Suddenly, all three were falling, tumbling over one another as the hallway dropped at a steep slant. They slid across the wooden floor, descending rapidly into yawning darkness.

CHAPTER 35

AS THEY PICKED themselves up, groaning, Dash glanced behind them. There was no sign of Dylan—not a footstep or an amber glow—and Dash realized that his brother could be anywhere. He turned back, and they started walking without a word.

Minutes later, they reached a crossroads. Three hallways stretched ahead of them. One was brightly lit with warm light, red-wood paneling along the bottom, and pinkish swirly wallpaper at the top. Another was pitch-dark and smelled like something rotting. And a third was illuminated by starlight, one wall of windows looking out on the meadow. A chorus of voices whispered from its far end. "All are welcome here . . . Everyone has a home at Larkspur . . . Even you . . ."

"This is the least fun fun house I've ever been in," said Poppy.

"You've been in a lot?" asked Azumi.

"Which way?" Dash interrupted, glancing back the way they'd come. "We need to stay on track."

"We know that, Dash," Azumi whispered. "We're in this together, remember?"

Dash grunted, staring down each new passage. "What if the house figured out we're searching for the scariest pathways? Maybe it's changed the rules of the game."

"We should stick to the plan," said Poppy.

"Okay, then." Dash pointed at the well-lit hall. "Is it weird that I feel most scared of this direction?"

"A little bit. But . . . if it's what scares you, maybe we should listen to that."

They headed toward the light.

"What's so scary about this, Dash?" asked Azumi.

"It makes me question my instincts," said Dash. "And I guess it makes me wonder if things can even go back to being normal. I'm not sure I can *handle* normal . . . not ever again."

The three walked in silence, passing by a sideboard where a colorful stained-glass Tiffany lamp sat like something you'd find in someone's kindly old grandmother's house.

"Still scared?" Poppy whispered.

Dash held up his flashlight. A closed door had appeared several steps in front of them. "Yup," he said, reaching for the knob. "Aren't you?"

The floor began to shudder.

"Wait!" said Poppy, a surge of terror flooding her veins.

But it was too late.

The door swung open and everything changed.

CHAPTER 36

POPPY IS STANDING at her bedroom window at Thursday's Hope, looking down at the sidewalk. A child is screaming several floors below, its voice echoing up the stairwell. A woman exits the building, wiping at her eyes, as if she's been crying. She steps into the crosswalk, but then she stops, her spine stiffening, as if she can feel Poppy's gaze. Turning, she glances up at the window, and Poppy recognizes her mother. The woman's pursed lips part. Poppy hears her voice in her head: *I'll be back! You're not safe with me! This is only for now.*

Poppy's vision blurs as tears fill her eyes. Her mother never hated her. She left her all those years ago to *protect* Poppy. She knew about Larkspur's curse, had run from it all her life.

Poppy remembers now. The screaming child downstairs is herself.

The woman raises a hand to wave as a black car pulls up beside her. One of the doors swings open, but the woman doesn't notice.

Poppy yells, bangs on the window, tries to warn her.

A long, pale arm reaches out from inside the car. It swings around the woman's waist, yanking her into the backseat. The door slams shut as the car peels off, leaving long black streaks on the asphalt.

Poppy's screams mix with the echoes ringing up from Ms. Tate's office downstairs.

Azumi steps into something damp. She's barefoot, dressed in her nightgown. She pulls her foot out of the mud and shakes it off. "Ew," she whispers. "What now?"

The air is cool and moist. It reminds her of home.

Glancing around, Azumi realizes that she *is* home. Back in the forest behind her house outside of Seattle. There is the old white elm she used to climb with Moriko when they were little. Her parents are calling to her, and she can see the beams of their flashlights cutting through the trees.

Azumi realizes that she's been sleepwalking again.

But Larkspur . . .

Was the whole thing a dream?

Azumi calls back. "Mommy! Daddy! I'm here!" She runs

toward them, leaping over fallen branches and moss-slick rocks. She knows the path well—she's walked it so many times.

"Azumi!" her father cries. "Not again!"

"I'm sorry! I was dreaming! It's okay, I'm safe!"

Her mother's warm arms envelop her. Her father's kisses wet her cheeks. Azumi is crying so hard that she shakes. Her parents rub her back until her sobbing slows, then lead her toward the house, where a spotlight shines from the back deck.

They climb the steps, and Azumi feels relief.

But then she notices something strange sitting in the middle of the deck: a small, square cage. The door swings open with a squeal. "What's this?" Azumi asks, her voice lost in the lengthening shadows. Her parents shove her toward the cage.

"It's our solution," says her mother flatly.

"We can't have another situation like your sister's," says her father. "Now get in."

Azumi shakes her head. "No . . . I don't want to."

Her mother's hands are strong. They push her to the ground. Her father's grip shoves her forward, and her knees burn as she scrapes them against the metal edge of the cage.

She's inside now, the walls and ceiling pressing tightly toward her. Before she can turn around, the door slams shut and a padlock closes on the latch. She clutches at the bars, shaking them, but they're solid. They don't move.

"Stop screaming, honey," her mother whispers, leaning close. "You'll attract the wolves."

In the woods, the growling has already begun.

In a field of the greenest grass, Dash peers down into a deep hole. At the bottom, a silver casket gleams in the sunlight. People all around him are dressed in black, holding handkerchiefs to their faces, sniffling. His parents stand on either side of him, hands on his shoulders, listening silently as the pastor reads a familiar passage.

The crowd starts to whisper.

"He was there, you know."

"I've heard he had something to do with it."

"I heard he's been in the psychiatric hospital."

"Poor Dylan. Such a good boy."

"They were so close. I wonder what happened?"

Dash covers his face, squeezing his eyes shut, wishing he could block out the voices.

But he doesn't have to. They stop on their own. Splaying his fingers, he sees that no one is watching him. No one is talking, except for the pastor, continuing his reading.

You're slipping away, D-Dash.

This voice is familiar.

You're not even really here. You know that, right? You're in a h-hospital room. You're unwell.

A face flashes into his mind. An old white man. A burn scar covering one eye.

Cyrus Caldwell.

It's all the experiments, says Cyrus. *You're finally broken. This is what it feels like. It's what the house wanted from you all along. Your fear. So tasty.* This last part is followed by a harsh slurping noise, like something licking enormous wet lips.

Dash thinks at the voice, *You don't scare me!*

Oh, no? There is a chuckle. *Just wait . . .*

Dash is suddenly alone, the grave yawning at his feet. Something is scratching from within the closed casket. A muffled voice calls out.

"Dylan!" Dash shouts back.

He leaps into the hole, tugging at the upper part of the coffin. It swings open.

But lying inside is Dylan's shriveled corpse. He isn't alive; he isn't trapped, or trying to get out. His lips are pulled back, revealing bleached, TV star teeth.

Dylan has been down here for a very long time.

"No! Dylan . . . please!" Dash yells until his throat hurts.

Laughter rings inside Dash's head. It's deeper than Cyrus's voice ever was.

The walls of the grave begin to tremble, the dirt shifting, pebbles dropping to the casket and then rolling off toward the bottom of the hole. Dash hugs himself, shaking his head over and over. "Dylan . . . Dylan . . . Dylan . . ." He says the name as if asking his brother for help.

Bony fingers claw out from the grave's walls. Dozens of skeletal hands burst forth, swiping at Dash. Instinctively, he ducks down, not realizing until it's too late how close he is to his brother's face.

Dylan's milky eyes swivel toward him. The dried lips twist into a wild sneer. His folded hands jolt up, clutching at Dash's face, chipped fingernails digging into Dash's skin.

Dash opens his mouth to scream, but Dylan shifts his grip, shoving his fingers deep inside. All Dash can do is choke as he struggles to breathe.

Think, Dash! Think!

This isn't right!

Dylan's fingers dance around inside his mouth.

How did you get here?

It's his brother's voice! It sounds very far away . . .

Get where? Dash answers.

Good question: Where are you?

In your grave!

Dylan's corpse leans its shriveled skull up from the casket pillow, jaw opening wide, teeth ready to bite.

No. You're not.

Then where . . . ?

Where . . .

The corpse's teeth snap shut right in front of Dash's face. Lightning flashes behind his eyes, and Dash realizes: *I'm in Larkspur House. I'm still in Larkspur!*

CHAPTER 37

THE CASKET BELOW him disappeared, and shadows encroached at the edge of his vision. He still couldn't breathe. Something heavy crushed his rib cage, and fingers were pressed against his mouth.

In the dim light, he made out a pale face hovering just above his own. Two amber orbs glowed from within dark eye sockets, and an exaggerated red smile grinned down at him.

"Dylan!" he managed to say. He tried to shift under his brother, but Dylan had him pinned tightly against the floor. The clown mask's smile only seemed to grow. "Dylan, listen to me! I *know* you're in there. I heard your voice . . . your *real* voice!"

The clown only laughed.

Dash turned his head back and forth. In his peripheral vision, he noticed that Poppy and Azumi were nearby. Poppy was by the window, pounding her fists against the glass. And Azumi was crouched on the floor, tucked into a ball.

The world around him grew darker.

Dash realized that the house was done with him. He was too big a risk to keep alive anymore. So it was ending him. How appropriate that the house should use the hands of his twin to do it.

And when the job was finished, the house would end the others too.

"D-Dylan . . . I-I love you . . . Forgive me."

The amber orbs dimmed for a moment. The clown's weight went slack.

Dash used all his strength to shove his brother off him. He scrambled backward, rising to his feet and running into the shadows. A wall of books appeared before him and he smacked into it, pain rocketing through his skull.

Looking back to the center of the room, he saw his brother stand up and glare at him. Dash's phone was lying on the floor nearby, the pale glow of its flashlight providing the room with its only source of light.

And even though it was faint, Dash recognized the space. The shelves behind him. The fireplace in the far wall. The broken musical instruments scattered across the floor. This was the room where they'd barricaded themselves against the Specials earlier that day—really, just that day?—where Marcus had given the boy in the dog mask his harmonica.

Dylan turned toward the girls. They appeared to be in their own little worlds, just as he'd been stuck in the grave, right before he'd snapped himself back into his body.

"Leave them alone!" Dash called out. "It's me you want."

"Oh, we want *all* of you," the deep voice rumbled from inside the clown mask. "We have to replace the ones you stole from us."

"But *you* stole them first! You stole all of us!"

The clown tilted its head as if confused. "Does a wolf cry over the deer in its claws? Does a fox weep for the rabbit in its teeth?" Its eyes glowed brighter. "Animals must eat. And so must we."

"You're evil!" Dash screamed.

The clown shook its head. "There is no such thing. Only nature." It moved closer to Azumi, who was still huddled on the floor, moaning in terror.

"Azumi!" Dash cried. "Whatever you're seeing . . . it's not real! Wake up! *Wake up!*"

Azumi shuddered and then raised her head. Dylan lurched toward her. "Watch out!" Dash shouted. He was too far away to stop him. But Azumi heard the warning. She rolled away as Dylan hit the floor beside her, then jumped to her feet. "Get to Poppy!" he called out.

Wide-eyed, Azumi bolted toward the window, grabbing Poppy's shoulder and spinning her away from the glass.

Poppy blinked and then looked around the room. She barely glanced at Dylan before her gaze swung toward the fireplace. She pointed, calling out, "There! That's the one!"

Dash was confused for only a moment. But when he looked where she was pointing, he noticed it too: the painting hanging over the mantel. The portrait of Consolida Caldwell stared back at them with golden eyes.

CHAPTER 38

"THERE!" POPPY CALLED out. "That's the one!"

It all made sense. Connie's signal in the mirror, running her fingers across her face. She'd been trying to tell Poppy that the painting she needed to find was the one of herself! It made so much sense. The necklace Connie wore in the painting was the same shape as the sigil she'd drawn onto the fogged-up mirror, a five-petaled flower. And Connie's eyes, usually hazel, were practically glowing. Just like the creature's.

"Help me," Poppy whispered to Azumi. They ran toward the mantel. Reaching up, the girls unhooked the frame and lowered it to the floor.

"Watch out!" Dash yelled, racing toward them from across the room.

Poppy turned to see Dylan crawling on his stomach like

some sort of salamander, slithering directly at them. The girls yelped as Dash jumped forward, catching his brother's heel, holding him in place. They hoisted up the portrait and ran away from the twins, hunkering down near the wall of books.

A deafening yowl erupted from behind Dylan's mask. He tried to kick Dash away, but Dash held tight, pinning him to the floor.

"Quick," said Poppy. "The turpentine."

Azumi reached into her pocket and pulled out the tin. "What do we do?"

Poppy took it from Azumi and tipped the tin upside down, letting the harsh liquid spill out onto the canvas. Layers of paint began to bubble up, colors melting and swirling together. The Girl's golden eyes streaked across her pale cheeks, crying shimmery tears.

Dylan shrieked as if someone had splattered him with acid. He battered at Dash, trying desperately to get up, to rescue the painting from the girls.

Paint continued to melt from the frame, puddling onto the floor below. Poppy cringed as layers of the Girl dissolved off the canvas. Another face seemed to appear—the woman from Poppy's dream, outside of Thursday's Hope.

Her mother.

Wide, tormented eyes stared up at her, as if begging Poppy to stop what was happening. Poppy started to reach for the canvas—*to do what? Save her?*—but Azumi caught her hands and made her look away from her mother's pleading expression.

The whole room shook. Books tumbled from the shelves, smacking against the floor like heavy hail during a summer storm.

Seconds later, raw fabric began to appear in the center of the frame. Blank canvas. A shape was singed into the taut cloth. That same five-pointed flower. Frederick's sigil. *Larkspur.*

He'd hidden the sigil here in plain sight, underneath a portrait of his daughter, whom he'd sacrificed to the creature for fame and glory.

If it was up to Poppy, no one would ever know the artist's name. Not ever again.

"The lighter," she whispered. Azumi handed it to her, and Poppy flipped open the lid, running her thumb over the flint until it sparked. A bud of flame began to blossom.

CHAPTER 39

FROM THE CORNER of his vision, Dash watched Poppy and Azumi spark the lighter. He held his brother, kicking and writhing, to keep Dylan from reaching them.

Dylan's cries were deafening. They rang in Dash's ears, threatening to burst his eardrums, as the room began rattling wildly.

It was working!

Soon, Dylan would be free too! Just like the Specials. All Dash had to do was hold on a little bit longer . . .

But then Dylan started to convulse, his whole body racked with spasms. Dash reached out for Dylan's mask, hoping he might finally be able to knock it away, but as his fingers made contact, white plastic shot across his skin like liquid, enveloping Dash's hands, binding them to his brother's face.

He tried to pull away, but pain flared up his arms. It felt as if his hands were being digested, melted from the inside.

"Help me!" he yelled.

Seconds later, Azumi was at his side, her face aghast. The white plastic was creeping up Dash's arms, stretching toward his elbows.

The clown mask's eyes burned bright with fury, as if to say *If I'm going, I'm taking you with me!*

Azumi grabbed Dash's shoulders and yanked him back. But Dylan came with him, flopping forward off the floor. "Poppy, hurry!" Azumi called out. "Burn the sigil!"

Poppy reached underneath the canvas and held the lighter steady. She watched as the canvas caught and then blackened, the flower symbol disappearing as a hole opened in the center, ringed by fire. The flame spread quickly to the edges of the frame, devouring the chemicals that had soaked into the fabric, and the heat bit at her fingers. Poppy dropped the frame. It smashed against the floor. The fire rose up from it like a spirit from a grave.

A heart-stopping sound, like nothing Poppy had ever heard, shook the room, buckling her knees. She hit the ground. The light and heat from the fire climbed through the air, up and up, until it licked at the ceiling, high above. And then it was suddenly sucked downward, as if into the canvas itself.

Cracks spread out from the plaster overhead, where the flame had touched. The floor shuddered again. Dash yelped in shock. Poppy crawled to him and Azumi and then gasped at what she saw.

Dash watched as the glow in Dylan's eyes winked out. His brother's body went limp, and the pain in Dash's hands and arms subsided. But the plastic still bound them.

"What happened?" Poppy asked, kneeling at his side. Her face was smudged with soot, but her eyes shone brightly, almost excited.

"He's stuck," said Azumi. "But we're going to get him out. Come on. Pull!" She continued to clutch at Dash's shoulders as Poppy held Dylan down.

"Don't hurt him!" Dash yelled, his eyes stinging with anger.

Overhead, the crackling plaster spread, dropping pieces of ceiling all around them. A black mark was growing from where Connie's portrait had fallen to the floor. Soon, it had crept underneath the spot where the four were sitting. The floor began to sag.

"We need to separate you two," said Azumi.

Azumi yanked him back, and Dash felt the plastic that coated him break away, crumbling from his hands and arms.

He nearly burst into tears when he saw that his fingers still had skin on them.

More important, though, was the clown mask clinging to his brother's face. This time, when Dash grabbed at it, the mask dropped to the floor, rocking back and forth, like the pendulum of a clock.

CHAPTER 40

DYLAN'S EYES WERE closed, but his eyelids fluttered as if he was dreaming.

Dash brushed at his brother's cheek, worried about what might happen when Dylan woke up. Would he flip out? Or had the Caldwell curse ended for good?

The wooden floor groaned beneath them. Dash could feel their weight pulling everyone down.

"This room isn't safe," said Azumi.

"Can we move him?" asked Poppy.

"Hold on a second," said Dash, his head spinning. He whispered, "Dylan? Dylan, wake up. Please. It's me. Dash."

The walls began to creak and crackle, as if the boards behind the plaster were breaking apart. There was a sudden jolt, and the room sank several inches at once. Azumi screamed and clutched Poppy's arm.

"Dash!" Poppy cried out.

"Just go!" Dash yelled. "If you're so scared, leave us!"

Poppy shrank back, hurt.

Pieces of the ceiling rained around them. The chandeliers wavered, scattering crystals. *Plink, plink, plink!*

Dylan's eyes blinked open. His brown irises shifted around the room and then zeroed in on his brother's face. "Dash? Is that you?"

Dash pulled his brother up from the floor and squeezed him so hard that Dylan cried out. "Please tell me that you're actually you," said Dash.

"Who—Who else would I be?"

"You don't remember?"

Dylan's mouth twisted into a frown. Of course he remembered. His lip quivered and his voice shook as he said, "I'm so sorry. My head . . . It got inside. The things it showed me . . . You have no idea." He glanced at Poppy. "I hurt you. I hurt all of you."

"It wasn't your fault," said Azumi, kneeling next to the boys.

Poppy stood rigidly beside her, looking terrified as the house crumbled.

Dylan grabbed Dash's shoulders and pushed him away, looking into his eyes. "It was, though." He sniffed. "In the woods, after that thing killed Marcus . . . I heard what you said." Glancing up at Poppy, he added, "What both of you said. That I was beyond saving. It made me mad. Madder than I've ever been. I think . . . I think I gave myself to it after that."

"I think we could all say the same," Azumi whispered.

Finally, Poppy crouched next to the others. "None of us chose this. Any of it."

"I get it now," said Dylan. "It's just . . . I was so scared to be alone here without you, Dash. I'm . . . I'm sorry I was such a horrible brother."

"I don't care what you were." Dash sniffed. "You're my best friend. Always. No matter what."

Poppy touched Dash's shoulder. "If we don't go now, we might not get another chance."

The floor dropped again. Cracks shot up the walls, widening like mouths gasping for breath. Dust and ash coughed out of the fireplace in a wide plume that stretched slowly toward the group.

Dash reached for his phone, the flashlight catching the dust, making it sparkle.

They stood, bracing themselves as the floor sloped toward the center. Jagged holes opened up beneath them, dropping chunks of crumbling wood into the darkness below. Clinging to one another, they raced to the door and through it, out into the hallway.

The mansion already seemed smaller. Farther down the

landing, a railing appeared. Stairs descended into the foyer. They were so much closer than they'd realized. Huddled together, they made their way to the first floor, the house quaking around them.

The walls were blackened now. After all, the place had been gutted by fires long ago. They were finally seeing the truth behind the house's mask. A harsh wind battered at the broken windows, making a strange wailing sound, as if the house itself were crying out in pain.

Whatever magic had been holding these ruins together was gone.

The group nearly tripped over the luggage that they'd left in the center of the parquet floor where they'd come together for the first time. Resounding booms belched from all the doorways as distant walls came tumbling down. The structure was trembling so violently, it was difficult for any of them to walk.

Staggering toward the double doors, they heard what sounded like thousands of voices calling to them.

Run!

Help!

Thank you!

Stay!

All of it mixed together in a nightmarish chorus. Poppy wondered if even though they'd destroyed Frederick Caldwell's pact, the thing that haunted this land was still here. Still angry. Still hungry.

The exit was only a few yards away.

The floor darkened as ashy rot spread under their feet, ready to disintegrate, to drop them down into the catacombs that had been built into the house's foundation.

Poppy flung herself across the threshold, and didn't stop running until she'd tumbled down the last few porch stairs and landed on the gravel driveway.

Azumi ran past her and then spun, looking back at the house. "Dash!" she cried out. "Dylan! Hurry!"

Poppy turned and saw the boys standing in the doorway. Dash was on the outside, Dylan on the inside, each reaching for the other, both shouting. Pieces of the vaulted ceiling were crashing to the floor of the foyer behind them. Dash gripped Dylan's hand and was yanking himself backward. But Dylan wasn't moving.

An invisible barrier had trapped him inside the house.

"Help us!" Dash cried out. The girls rushed back to the entry. They grabbed Dash around the waist and pulled, throwing themselves toward the driveway. But it didn't work. The three stared into Dylan's horrified face as he continued to stand in the opening.

"It won't let me leave!" Dylan cried.

CHAPTER 41

"BUT WHY?" ASKED Poppy. "We destroyed the sigil."

"We broke Frederick's pact," said Dash. "But the creature is holding him here."

Poppy gasped. "We need to give him something to set him free. Something that was taken from him. Like how we saved the Specials."

Dylan blinked. "Nobody took anything from me."

Dash shivered. "Yes, someone did," he said. The others stared at him. The house continued to rumble as large chunks of its walls crumbled around its periphery. "I took your life. Back in Los Angeles. My prank—"

Dylan's breath hitched. "But that was an accident. You didn't mean to."

Everyone stood in silence for a moment.

"How are you supposed to give his life back?" asked Azumi. She looked into the foyer, and then shouted, "It's not fair!" She almost expected a growling laugh to answer her, but all that came was the sound of more destruction.

"There's got to be something we can do," said Poppy. "Maybe—"

Dash stepped across the threshold and stood beside his brother.

Poppy flinched. "Dash, get out of there. It could collapse at any second."

Dash shook his head. "I won't leave him alone again. Not here."

Azumi reached for them. "But you'll die!"

"I won't leave him."

Dylan shoved at Dash. "No! You can't!"

"You don't get to tell me what to do. No one gets to tell me what to do anymore." He stared into Poppy's eyes. "This is what *I* need. Please don't take it from me."

The floor cracked open behind the boys. Dust and ash rose up in clouds.

Dash grabbed at the doors and swung them together. Just before he pushed them shut, he yelled out to the girls, "Run!"

Poppy stood her ground. She rattled the handles and then pounded on the wood. But the doors would not budge. "We've already made it out, Dash! We beat it! Don't do this to yourself!" The stone wall began to tremble.

"You'll be crushed, Poppy!" Azumi shouted. She yanked on Poppy's arm, dragging her down the front steps and across the gravel.

They paused twenty yards from the mansion, out where the driveway circled around on itself. Looking back, they watched the spires of Larkspur House tilt and tumble, its walls and towers turning to rubble as the first light of dawn began to erase the stars in the dark sky far beyond.

CHAPTER 42

DASH AND DYLAN sat huddled at the bottom of the steps in the foyer. Cross-legged, they faced each other, holding hands.

Boom! Another piece of the ceiling punched a wide hole in the floor several feet away.

Dash examined his brother's face, looking for the details that had always distinguished them from each other: the way Dylan's left eyebrow rose higher than his right, the scar under Dylan's bottom lip from when he'd fallen from his high chair as an infant. Dash knew that if they were to stare at each other for the rest of eternity, they'd find so many differences between them that they wouldn't even be able to recognize themselves as twins.

Tears dangled from the end of Dylan's nose. "I didn't know that ghosts could cry," said Dash.

Dylan smiled briefly before his face crumpled. "You don't deserve this," he said, his voice choked.

"I know," said Dash. "But neither do you."

The stained-glass windows near the ceiling shattered, and colored shards rained down. The floor vibrated, and the center opened up like a bull's-eye. The luggage that had been sitting there all day plunged into the catacomb's depths. Large stones tumbled down from atop the double doors, just missing the boys.

Dylan lunged forward and threw his arms around Dash, as if he could protect him.

"I wish we'd said good-bye to Mom and Dad," said Dash, trying to ignore everything but his brother. "Will they ever find out what happened to us?"

Dylan sniffed. "Well, they already know what happened to me."

Dash nodded. "Right. I guess I'll be the mystery."

A great whooshing sound echoed from the top of the stairs, as if all the air were being sucked out of the building. Something was coming. Something large and dark and unforgiving.

"Will it hurt?" Dash whispered.

Dylan shook his head. "I don't know."

"If you can't remember," said Dash, "then maybe it doesn't matter." Something wrenched at the ceiling. An enormous piece of it dropped inward with a shriek, bringing several dozen rafters with it. Dash yelped.

Dylan squeezed his hands. "Thank you, Dash."

"For what?"

"For giving me what I needed."

Dash shuddered, confused. "But I didn't—" He stopped talking. Dylan had started to fade, his skin growing transparent, his touch cool instead of warm. "What's happening?"

But Dash knew. He understood. It was time. Finally.

Dylan's voice whispered, "Go. Hurry."

His lips parted, his teeth gleaming in the dark and dusty space. A smile. A real one. Genuine. Happy. It lingered in the air for a few seconds, even after the rest of his body had gone away. Then it too disintegrated into nothing.

Dash stood on trembling legs, the house rumbling in its final throes. The rushing sound at the top of the stair grew louder, like a storm approaching, a wall of wind ready to clear a path of destruction.

A black pit opened just inches from where he stood. Looking down, Dash could see bleached skulls staring up at him from the shadowed crypts.

He leapt up the stone steps, finding solid ground by the double doors. Yanking desperately at the handles, he cried out, "Dylan! Help me!" But the doors wouldn't give. And Dylan didn't answer. Dash shrieked in anger and terror as Larkspur's walls toppled around him.

CHAPTER 43

POPPY AND AZUMI stared in awe as a cloud of smoke and dust rose up from the wreckage.

When the haze began to lift, lit pink by the coming sun, Larkspur's remains stood out in silhouette. The roof was gone. Patches of stone wall marked where the sprawling foundation had been buried, with green saplings and thick brush growing through the gaps. Brick archways were all that was left of old doorways and windows. Almost a dozen chimneys stood over it all like watchtowers at a prison.

Poppy didn't realize that she was holding Azumi's hand until Azumi let go and dropped to the ground, weeping. Poppy felt strangely empty. This place was supposed to have been her new home. But now she couldn't imagine ever living here. And the poor people who had . . .

Birds in the distance chattered and sang, awakened by the dawn. A soft breeze rustled the brush in the ruins and blew her mess of hair out of her face.

"Connie?" Poppy whispered. "Are you still here?" Part of her hoped that the house had released its hold on the Girl, but she worried about what life might hand her next and how she would survive without her old friend. Connie didn't answer.

Someone else did.

"Help . . . me . . ."

The voice was so soft that Poppy wondered if she'd imagined it. It called out again. This time, it was clear that it was buried under the pile of rocks.

"Dash!" Azumi yelled. She ran past Poppy, leaping up the stone steps and over mounds of debris.

Shocked, Poppy chased after her, wondering if they were both still under the house's spell.

A bruised hand reached up from around the side of a wide, broken door. "Poppy! Get over here! He's alive!"

The girls worked furiously, tossing rocks out of the way, uncovering the doors that had fallen end to end and protected Dash from being crushed. They pulled him free to find that, miraculously, he was covered with only small cuts and bruises.

Sitting up, he burst into tears. Poppy and Azumi leaned back and let him cry.

Dash told them what had happened as the house came down—how Dylan had disappeared, freed from Larkspur's clutches.

Freed from Dash's own need to keep him close.

After they caught their breath, they scrambled away from the ruins, making their way back to the gravel driveway. There was nothing left for them to do but follow the path down the hill and into the woods. They walked quickly, not speaking of what they'd do if they found the gate closed again.

In fact, they didn't speak much at all.

Azumi stepped into the shadowed forest, half expecting the trees from the base of Mount Fuji to rise up around her and send her back into the middle of her nightmares. But the birds continued to sing. Daylight was breaking through the branches overhead.

She thought of her parents, suddenly unsure why they'd allowed her to travel alone to a school they'd never actually visited themselves. Had they been under Larkspur's spell? Or did they really believe that Azumi would be safe?

What would she tell them? That a haunted house had lured her across the country and then tried to eat her? That she'd made contact with her dead sister? That she'd nearly gone crazy?

Or maybe she'd come up with another story. Something easier to believe. Something that wouldn't give them nightmares. The big question, however, was this: Would the story give Azumi nightmares? Would she keep walking at night?

Would the voices continue?

Or had Larkspur made her stronger?

Poppy and Dash strolled ahead of her, his arm thrown over her shoulder. It helped Azumi to know that she wouldn't be alone with the memories of this place. She knew that these two would be there whenever she needed them. Probably forever.

Azumi peered up the driveway, wishing that Moriko—the *real* Moriko—would appear one last time.

Leave the path, Azumi. Get out. Run . . .

How easy it was to get lost.

The path . . .

Azumi sighed and swiped at her eyes, thankful that this one would lead her home.

Dash limped down the gravel driveway. Poppy helped him along, steering him around potholes and lumpy weeds.

He thought of his brother. Of his smile fading into shadow.

He remembered now. The accident. The funeral. The hospital. Everything was clear. They weren't pleasant memories, but at least they were there. Destroying Frederick Caldwell's sigil had not only ended the creature's pact, but also its hold on Dash's mind.

He thought of Marcus and Azumi and Poppy.

If each of them had been called to Larkspur because of their connection with the dead, Dash felt like that connection had been severed.

A blessing and a curse.

Dylan was gone for good.

No more pretending. No more pranks or games.

Maybe when he got back to LA, his parents would see that he was better. That he was healing. Or that at least he was willing to try.

The morning was cool. Dew clung to Poppy's arms and shoulders. She walked with purpose, her head held high, her eyes focused forward.

But her mind raced as she laid out plans.

She would not return to Thursday's Hope. At least not right away.

Once the group made it back to town, she'd ask Azumi if there was an extra bed in her family's house. Maybe she could stay there for awhile. If Azumi said no, Dash's parents might be able to help out. And if not there . . . she'd go somewhere else. There were plenty of options.

But the next step wasn't the most important part. Whatever happened to her after this would only help Poppy reach her final destination. Her mother.

Poppy understood why her mother had left her at Thursday's Hope all those years ago. She'd believed in the Caldwell curse. She'd been trying to protect Poppy from whatever she'd believed was chasing her. How wonderful it would be to tell her mother that she'd defeated it, to let her know that they were safe now.

They could be together. They didn't have to hide anymore.

Poppy thought of Connie and Marcus and Dylan. She thought of *all* the souls who'd been caught in the creature's web: the Specials, the first orphans, the medium's wards, the young explorers from Greencliffe.

Her own family had set up the web in the first place. It felt right that she'd been the one to tear it down. To set everyone free.

Poppy was free now too.

She took Dash's arm and hiked it higher on her shoulder. He glanced at her and smiled.

"Look!" said Azumi, pointing forward.

Ahead, the stone wall appeared through the trees. At the spot where it intersected the driveway, the gate was open.

Poppy could see the road on the other side and the woods

beyond, and she whooped with joy. Azumi and Dash joined her. It made her feel wild and a bit dizzy.

The group rushed forward, stopping just at the threshold of the opening, peering down the hill, where the rooftops of Greencliffe peeked up through the trees. The Hudson River glimmered in the distance, reflecting a violet sky over the horizon.

Poppy, Azumi, and Dash grabbed one another's hands. Together, they stepped through Larkspur's broken gate and out onto Hardscrabble Road.

ART CREDITS

ENDPAPERS

Endpaper photos ©: 2–3: wallpaper: A_l.i.s_A/Shutterstock, flower wallpaper: jannoon028/Shutterstock; 6–7: Shadow House illustration: Shane Rebenschied for Scholastic; mansion: Dariush M/Shutterstock, fog: Maxim van Asseldonk/Shutterstock, clouds: Aon_Skynotlimit/Shutterstock, grass and trees: Maxim van Asseldonk/Shutterstock.

INTERIOR

Interior photos ©: 18: balloon clown: Comstock/Getty Images, balloon clown face: nito/Shutterstock, raised arm clown: Ljupco/Getty Images, raised arm clown face: Alex Malikov/Shutterstock, clown with bows: Elnur/Shutterstock, far left clown: sdominick/Getty Images, far left face: Jeff Cameron Collingwood/Shutterstock, far right clown: sdominick/Getty Images, far right face: Alex Malikov/Shutterstock, clown hat: Charice Silverman for Scholastic, tents: Westend61 Premium/Shutterstock, 59: woman with tilted head: Andriy Blokhin/Shutterstock, woman with hair draped: Kamenetskiy Konstantin/Shutterstock, woman from back: Kamenetskiy Konstantin/Shutterstock, woman shaking head: KatarinaDj/Shutterstock, poses: Keirsten Geise for Scholastic, foreground: sturti/Getty Images; 89: wreckage: StockPhotosLV/Shutterstock, car: Grafissimo/Getty Images, interior: Tiramisu Studio/Shutterstock, wall: boonyarak voranimmanont/Shutterstock, ladder: Meng Luen/Shutterstock, ghost: Gemenacom/Shutterstock; 114: shed: Brad Remy/Shutterstock, sky and grass: Dudarev Mikhail/Shutterstock, forest: Evannovostro/Shutterstock, lightning: Charice Silverman for Scholastic; 124–125: paths: PhotoRoman/Shutterstock, landscape: Mike Pellinni/Shutterstock, Great Wall: fotoVoyager/Getty Images, sky: Igor Kovalchuk/Shutterstock, mansion: Dariush M/Shutterstock, fog: Maxim van Asseldonk/Shutterstock, clouds: Aon_Skynotlimit/Shutterstock, mansion composite: Shane Rebenschied for Scholastic; 141: path: Textures.com, skull: witoon214/Shutterstock, big bones: Photographicss/Shutterstock, small bones: Picsfive/Shutterstock, shoe: Keirsten Geise for Scholastic; 164: hand: Viacheslav Blizniuk/Shutterstock, sofa: PinkyWinky/Shutterstock, frame: CG Textures, glass and composite: Charice Silverman for Scholastic; 169: room: Library of Congress, painting top right: CG Textures, painting on easel: CG Textures, easel: frescomovie/Shutterstock, Matilda: Larry Rostant for Scholastic, cat mask: CSA Plastock/Getty Images; doll: unclepepin/Shutterstock, carpet: CG Textures; 193: wallpaper: Larysa Kryvoviaz/Shutterstock, girl: robangel69/Fotolia, frame: Chatchawan/Shutterstock, melting effect: Charice Silverman for Scholastic; mantle: Zick Svift/Shutterstock, photo and clock: CG Textures; 213: chimney: T W Brinton/Shutterstock, iris: Lopatin Anton/Shutterstock.

About the Author

Dan Poblocki is the author of several books for young readers, including *The House on Stone's Throw Island*, *The Book of Bad Things*, *The Nightmarys*, *The Stone Child*, and the Mysterious Four series. His recent novels, *The Ghost of Graylock* and *The Haunting of Gabriel Ashe*, were both Junior Library Guild selections and made the American Library Association's Best Fiction for Young Adults list in 2013 and 2014. Dan lives in New York in an apartment where the ghosts, thankfully, are the quiet kind. Visit him online at www.danpoblocki.com.

DON'T MISS ANY OF THE CHILLING ADVENTURES!

Step into Shadow House.

Enter Shadow House

Each image in the book reveals a haunting in the app.

Search out hidden sigils ◊ in the book for bonus scares in the app.

Step into ghost stories, where the choices you make determine your fate.

CAN YOU ESCAPE?